U0095752

普通高校应用型人才培养规划教材

视听说英语教程

（学生用书）

主　编　王秀珍
副主编　徐　江　宁克建
参　编　李　琳　孙　言　徐　玮
　　　　唐湘茜　张琼尹　王　燕
　　　　戴　雷　濮　琼

经济科学出版社

图书在版编目（CIP）数据

视听说英语教程（学生用书）/王秀珍主编．—北京：经济科学出版社，2009.8
·普通高校应用型人才培养规划教材
ISBN 978 - 7 - 5058 - 8546 - 2

Ⅰ．视… Ⅱ．王… Ⅲ．英语—听说教学—高等学校—教材 Ⅳ．H319.9

中国版本图书馆 CIP 数据核字（2009）第 152274 号

责任编辑：范 莹 肖 萍
责任校对：刘 昕
技术编辑：董永亭

视听说英语教程（学生用书）
王秀珍 主编
经济科学出版社出版、发行 新华书店经销
社址：北京市海淀区阜成路甲 28 号 邮编：100142
编辑部电话：88191417 发行部电话：88191540
网址：www. esp. com. cn
电子邮箱：esp@ esp. com. cn
北京欣舒印务有限公司印刷
华丰装订厂装订
787 × 1092 16 开 15.5 印张 400000 字
2009 年 9 月第 1 版 2009 年 9 月第 1 次印刷
印数：0001 - 2000 册
ISBN 978 - 7 - 5058 - 8546 - 2 定价：24.00 元

普通高校应用型人才培养规划教材
编 审 委 员 会

主任委员：

    甘德安

委 员（以姓氏笔画为序）：

    万玲莉　王秀珍　王超英　李立慧　何炜煌　余超波
    欧阳仲威　皇甫积庆　崔正华　谢建群　黄镇宇

总　序

经过几年的快速发展，我国教育已进入高等教育大国的行列，按照党的十七大精神，向建设人力资源强国迈进。数以千万计的学生在各级、各类高等学校学习各种知识和培养能力，为成为社会主义的建设者和新时期的应用型人才而努力。高等教育从"精英化"到"大众化"的转变，除了数量的扩大外，必须在培养目标、教学内容、教学方法、教材等方面进行改革，以适应培养不同类型人才和不同类型高校的教学需要。

独立学院自开办以来，在教学各方面，特别是教材基本沿用了普通本科的教学资源，这给特色教育和定向教学带来了诸多不便，难以达到教委设定的教学目的。有鉴于此，我们在"服务于地方，培养应用型人才"这一总的目标指导下，组织了一批教学经验丰富、致力于教学改革研究、在相关课程方面有较深造诣的教师，按教育部的教育培养规划，编写了这套适合独立学院本科教学的系列教材，旨在有针对性地培养应用型高等学历人才，因此我们称这套教材为"普通高校应用型人才培养规划教材"。

我们编写这套教材的基本思想是：对基本原理、基本理论，重在结论和应用。理论部分遵循教学大纲，不求深入全面，但求适用，对相关理论做必要的引介。书中编列了较多的例子和习题，增加了学生自我训练、独立解题的素材，期望帮助学生加深对理论知识的理解和应用。我们力求这套丛书在内容结构上既区别于传统本科教材，又不同于高职高专教材。在理论知识方面既有一定的系统性，也兼顾了现代性；既注重知识间的逻辑性，也突出了知识的应用性；在够用、实用、适用的前提下，还编入一些有深度知识的链接，供要求进一步提高的学生自学之用。本套教材在文字上力求准确易懂，适当增加例图，有较好的可读性，便于学生自学。

由于我们的水平有限，书中难免出现一些问题，敬请各位教师和广大学生给予细心的指正和热情的帮助。在此，对于大力支持这套教材出版发行的经济科学出版社也一并表示真诚的感谢。

教材编审委员会

甘德安

2008 年 1 月

前言

　　《英语视听说教程》是一套根据新的教学理念，集视、听、说于一体的适合于独立学院英语专业学生入学阶段强化训练的教材。旨在让学生接受与中学阶段完全不同的英语学习方式，为后期的英语教学做一个过渡和铺垫。本教材分为学生用书和教师用书各一册。

　　《英语视听说教程》（学生用书）分为Pare one (以视听为主)和Part Two (以视说为主)。每个部分分为12个主题，即Greetings and Introduction（自我介绍与问候），Good Manners（礼仪），Confidence（自信），Gratitude（感恩），College Life（大学生活），Networks（网络），Western Festivals（西方节日），Environmental Protection（环境保护），Olympics（奥运），Tuition and Part-time Jobs（学费与兼职），Earthquakes（地震） and Manned Space Shuttle（载人航天）。编写形式有：Preview Exercises（视听预习）；Warming up Exercises（热身练习）；Listening Material/Listening Material Review（听力视说练习）；Additional Listening Material/Additional Listening Material Review (补充听力视说练习)；Video-aural Material / Video-aural Material Review （视听视说练习）；Additional Video-aural Material （补充视说练习）；Listening Skills (听力技能练习)；Phonetics Tips（语音训练）。

　　本教材主要特点有如下几个方面：

　　Preview exercises（视听预习）部分，是专门为学生课前预习设计的。学生通过自行听写、回答相关问题，观看与本单元主题相关的一段视频画面后，就能轻松进行课前预习，为课堂上师生互动打下基础。

Listening Material/Listening Material Review（听力视说练习）部分，一段听力材料播放三四遍，第一遍训练抓大意，第二遍训练听细节，第三遍对部分材料做听写训练（精听训练），另外在视说课中教师还将对视听的材料进行口语表达训练，帮助学生熟悉理解材料，使听力和口语得到提高。

另外，本书还结合相关外语类的水平考试，专门开辟了听力技巧讲解和训练专栏，通过精讲多练，以达到提高学生听力理解能力的目的。除此之外，我们还把语音训练作为一个重要环节列入了本教材，旨在帮助学生掌握重要的语音训练方法，使学生能在老师的引导下进行有效的训练，为今后的英语学习打下良好的语音基础。

本教材内容可安排96学时，为期8周时间完成。具体做法是：每周12学时，其中视听6学时，视说4学时，语音2学时。该学时安排的框架在使用过程中可根据各校具体情况自行调整。

编写者均为视听、视说、语音课的任课教师，通过实践，他们积累了较丰富的经验。而本教材正是各位教师教学理念、教学方法、教学研究的集体结晶。

由于编写者水平和经验有限，教材中难免还有不足之处，希望各位读者不吝赐教。

编　者
2009年8月

CONTENTS

Part one

CONTENTS

CONTENTS

Part two

CONTENTS

PART ONE
Viewing and Listening

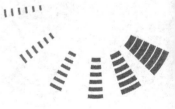

PART ONE
Viewing and Listening

I

Preview Exercises

1. Dictation:

Directions: *Listen and dictate what you've heard.*

_____

_____

_____

_____

_____

2. Questions:

(1) What are they doing?

_____

_____

_____

_____

(2) Would you introduce yourself briefly?

_____

_____

_____

_____

_____

II

Warming up Exercises

Background knowledge

1. Culture difference in greetings
2. An introduction to the ways of greetings
3. Different ways of introduction
4. Check the preview exercises

Listening Material

Directions: *In this part, you are going to listen to a conversation. When you listen to the conversation for the first time, you should pay attention to its main ideas and answer some general comprehension questions. When you listen for the second time, you should focus on important details and answer some specific comprehension questions. When the conversation is repeated for the third and fourth time, you should complete the dictation task.*

Glossary

（1）journalist   *n.* 记者   （3）occupation   *n.* 职业
（2）interview   *n./v.* 面试,采访

Task 1

◁ *Now listen to the conversation for the first time and answer questions 1 to 2.*

（1）What are the woman and man doing before the telephone rings?

    A. They are introducing themselves.

    B. The woman is introducing her parents.

    C. The woman is showing her family album.

    D. They are introducing each other's family.

（2）What does the telephone call tell us?

    A. It is about an appointment.

    B. It is about an introduction to a company.

    C. It is about an personal information.

    D. It is about an interview.

Task 2

◁ *Now listen to the conversation for the second time and answer questions 3 to 5.*

（3）Where is her mother from?

    A. England.   B. America.   C. Mexico.   D. France.

(4) Please write down the jobs in the blanks.

Denis is a(n) _____.

Dan is a(n) _____.

Peter is a(n) _____.

Joe is a(n) _____.

Jack is a(n) _____.

Bill is a(n) _____.

(5) What job interview does she want to take?

A. A journalist.　　B. A singer.　　C. A teacher.　　D. Not given.

Task 3

🔊 *Now listen to the conversation twice and complete the dictation task by filling in the blanks numbered 1 to 5 with the exact words. At the end of this task, there will be a pause for you to check what you've written.*

Excuse me. Hello! Hi, Carrol, how are you? I'm fine, thanks. It's Carrol. (1) _____ information? OK. I'm 25 years old. My middle name is Ana, Susan Ana Webster. It (2) _____ Ana, a-n-a. My phone number is (3) _____. My address is 340 Ocean Drive. OK? Oh, Carrol, what's your phone number? (4) _____. OK. Yes. An interview? What time? Who's that? What's her (5) _____? Oh, OK. Thanks. See you tomorrow. Goodbye.

IV　Additional Listening Material

Directions: *In this part, you are going to listen to a short passage. When you listen to this passage for the first time, you should pay attention to its main ideas and answer some general comprehension questions. When you listen for the second time, you should focus on important details and answer some specific comprehension questions. When the passage is repeated for the third and fourth time, you should complete the dictation task.*

🔊 *Now listen to the passage for the first time and answer questions 1 to 2.*

(1) What do we know about her work?

    A. She is a good police officer.

    B. She is both a police officer and a singer.

    C. She works only on weekdays.

    D. She works regularly.

(2) What can we learn from the self-introduction?

    A. She works very hard.

    B. She likes her family.

    C. Her life is dull.

    D. Her life is colorful.

Task 2

🔊 *Now listen to the passage for the second time and answer questions 3 to 5.*

(3) How many people are there in her family?

    A. Five.   B. Six.   C. Four.   D. Three.

(4) What does she often do in her spare time?

    A. She works as a policewoman.

    B. She works as a singer.

    C. She works as a cook.

    D. She works as a driver.

(5) According to the self-introduction, which of the following is true?

    A. Every day is the same to her.

    B. Every night on weekdays she talks with her parents.

    C. She has three days' working as a singer.

    D. She often has three meals with her family.

Task 3

🔊 *Now listen to this passage twice and complete the dictation task by filling in the blanks numbered 1 to 7 with the exact words or sentences with exact words. At the end of this task, there will be a pause for you to check what you've written.*

Weekday nights I stay at home. I eat (1) _____, I (2) _____, I (3) _____ TV. I (4) _____ with Susan. Every night is the (5) _____. But weekends are (6) _____. Friday, Saturday and Sunday I (7) _____ at Ivories (娱乐场所的名字). I start at 9 o'clock. I am a singer. But on Monday, I am a police officer.

V | Video-aural Material

Directions: *In this part, you are going to watch a video clip. When you watch the video for the first time, you should pay attention to its main idea and answer some general comprehension questions. When the clip is played for the second time, you should focus on important details and answer some specific comprehension questions. When the clip is repeated for the third and fourth time, you should complete the sentences with the words or phrases you have heard in the news.*

Task 1

👁 *Now watch the video for the first time and answer questions 1 to 2.*

(1) What are they doing?

    A. They are greeting and talking to each other.

    B. They are working and reading together.

    C. They are greeting and introducing each other.

    D. They are playing and drinking together.

(2) Where does this conversation take place?

    A. In an office.   B. At a bar.

    C. In a TV station.   D. In a radio station.

Task 2

👁 *Now watch the clip for the second time and answer questions 3 to 5.*

(3) What is the relationship between the men and women?

    A. They are hosts.

    B. They are friends.

    C. They are clerks.

    D. They are new colleagues.

(4) When do they greet to each other?

    A. In the morning.   B. After the work.

    C. Before the work.   D. While meeting.

(5) What can we infer from this conversation?

    A. Everybody here is the host.

    B. Susan is still single.

    C. Jack is very interesting.

    D. Carol is very kind.

Task 3

👁 *Now watch the video twice and complete the sentences by filling in the blanks numbered 1 to 6 with the words and phrases you have just heard in the news. At the end of this task, there will be a pause for you to check what you've written.*

(1) I'm Susan Webster. It's nice to _____ you, Carol.

(2) This is the _____ for the host.

(3) This _____ says I am the host.

(4) She is Linda Marino? Really? She is very _____.

(5) Susan, it's nice to meet you. What's your _____ name?

(6) _____. Susan Webster?

VI Listening Skills

1. The skills of short conversations(1)

"Short conversations" is a common testing item in listening comprehension. It seems easy, but it is also difficult to get full marks. This is because the conversation belongs to one-round conversation. It goes too fast to be grasped fully in meaning. Therefore, mastering proper listening skills can help you much to avoid the unnecessary loss.

(1) Scan the four choices to have the information in mind.

(2) Guess the main content about the conversation.

(3) Predict the questions.

(4) Catch some related information, such as date, figure and name.

(5) Read the four choices again and choose the right one.

(6) Practice listening to different types of conversations and get familiar with the ways of talking.

2. Sample practice

Directions: *In this section you will hear 12 short conversations. At the end of each conversation a question will be asked about what was said. Both the conversation and the question will be spoken only once. After each question there will be a pause. During the pause you must read the four choices marked A, B, C, and D, and decide which is the best answer.*

(1) A. 25 pounds.　　B. 20 pounds.　　C. 205 pounds.　　D. 225 pounds.

(2) A. Dentist.　　B. Physician.　　C. Physicist.　　D. Surgeon.

(3) A. An attendant.　B. A customer.　　C. A boss.　　D. A driver.

(4) A. Korea.   B. South Korea.   C. Seoul.   D. France.

(5) A. She will listen to the music.   B. She will go to the market.

     C. She will buy a new TV.   D. She will fix it by herself.

(6) A. He was very sad.   B. He was very angry.

     C. He was very nervous.   D. He was very happy.

(7) A. He was badly injured.   B. He fell down from the car.

     C. He lost his seat belt.   D. He was slightly hurt.

(8) A. Dr. Lemon is waiting for a patient.

     B. Dr. Lemon is busy at the moment.

     C. Dr. Lemon has lost his patient.

     D. Dr. Lemon has gone out to visit a patient.

(9) A. He doesn't enjoy business trips as much as he used to.

     B. He doesn't think he is capable of doing the job.

     C. He thinks the pay is too low to support his family.

     D. He wants to spend more time with his family.

(10) A. A mystery story.

     B. The hiring of a shop assistant.

     C. The research for a reliable witness.

     D. An unsolved case of robbery.

(11) A. Prof. Kennedy is very happy to help her.

     B. She is very sorry to trouble him now.

     C. Prof. Kennedy is not a hardworking man.

     D. She is very happy to be his student.

(12) A. The woman feels sorry for the man.

     B. The man is a member of the staff.

     C. The area is for passengers only.

     D. The woman is asking the man to leave.

3. Additional training

Directions: *In this section, you will hear 10 short conversations. At the end of each conversation, a question will be asked about what was said. Both the conversation and the question will be spoken only once. After each question there will be a pause. During the pause, you must read the four choices marked A, B, C and D, and decide which is the best answer.*

(1) A. A math teacher and his colleague.

B. A teacher and his student.

C. A student and his classmate.

D. A librarian and a student.

(2) A. Tony could not continue the experiment.

B. Tony finished the experiment last night.

C. Tony thought the experiment was well done.

D. Tony had expected the experiment to be easier.

(3) A. She can't put up with the noise.

B. She wants to save money to buy a piano.

C. The present apartment is too expensive.

D. She has found a job in a neighboring area.

(4) A. He is not very enthusiastic about his English lessons.

B. He has made great progress in his English.

C. He is a student of the music department.

D. He is not very interested in English songs.

(5) A. At home.   B. In a restaurant.

C. In a car.   D. On the street.

(6) A. His injury kept him at home.   B. He didn't think it necessary.

C. He was too weak to see the doctor.   D. He failed to make an appointment.

(7) A. 5:15.   B. 5:10.   C. 4:30.   D. 5:00.

(8) A. The man needs help.   B. The man is complaining.

C. The man likes his job.   D. The man is talking with his boss.

(9) A. Wear a new dress.   B. Make a silk dress.

C. Attend a party.   D. Go shopping.

(10) A. He played his part quite well.

B. He preformed better than the secretary.

C. He worked well enough.

D. He exaggerated his part.

Unit Two Good Manners

Preview Exercises

1. Dictation:

Directions: *Fill in the blanks while listening.*

An estimated 22 percent of American high school _____ smoke, and according to Cathy Backinger, chief of the _____ Control Research Branch at the National Cancer Institute in the United States, approximately _____ of young smokers will eventually _____ _____ from a smoking-related illness.

2. Questions:

(1) Do you think smoking in public is a good manner or bad one? Why?

_____

_____

_____

_____

_____

(2) Please tell us what manners you appreciate in the college.

_____

_____

_____

_____

_____

Warming up Exercises

Background knowledge

1. An Introduction to table manners

In most Western restaurants and homes there are rules about how to talk, eat and sit that are highly restrictive, and they create an atmosphere that is completely different from what we find here in China. As for eating, westerners do it quietly. No eating noises are allowed. Everything must be done as quietly as possible. Therefore, we have to eat with our mouths closed. To make a "smacking" noise is, perhaps, the worst offence possible. While drinking soup or coffee or wine "slurping" is also forbidden. With that in mind, it is, of course, unthinkable to speak with one's mouth full of food.

2. An Introduction to good manners

Good manners are very important for all of us. Trying to be polite and friendly to others will help us get respects from others. As college students, we should do some small things in front of us right now, because we must know it is our duty to make our college more beautiful than before. The following is the good manners we should follow.

(1) Good manners in college
    ① Keep the timetable.
    ② Listen to teachers attentively.
    ③ Be economical.
    ④ Show your concern for your classmates.
    ⑤ Keep the rules of the college.
    ⑥ Respect your teachers.

(2) Good manners at home
    ① Respect the family members.
    ② Help parents do the housework.
    ③ Follow the table manners.
    ④ Be polite to your neighbors.
    ⑤ Throw rubbish in the fixed place.
    ⑥ Serve your relatives and friends in a friendly way.

3. Check the preview exercises

Listening Material

Directions: *In this part, you are going to listen to a program. When you listen to this program for the first time, you should pay attention to its main ideas and answer some general comprehension questions. When you listen for the second time, you should focus on important details and answer some specific comprehension questions. When the program is repeated for the third time, you should complete the dictation task.*

Glossary

(1) formal *adj.* 正式的	(4) casual *adj.* 随意的
(2) rude *adj.* 粗鲁的	(5) cutlery *adj.* 刀具的
(3) personally *adv.* 个人地	(6) panic *adj.* 恐慌的

Task 1

🔊 *Now listen to the program for the first time and answer questions 1 to 2.*

(1) What does this program tell us?

  A. A piece of BBC news.   B. A formal dinner.

  C. A casual dinner.   D. Table manners.

(2) What can we do well when you are at a dinner table?

  A. We have to respect the host and hostess.

  B. We should help the host and hostess to do cooking.

  C. We should learn something from the host and hostess.

  D. We have to follow what they tell us.

Task 2

🔊 *Now listen to the program for the second time and answer questions 3 to 5.*

(3) Which of the following is one of the good table manners?

  A. Don't speak while eating.

B. Put your elbows on the table in formal dinner.

C. Use your forks or spoons exchangeablly.

D. Don't eat until the host begins eating.

(4) What does "cutlery set" mean?

A. Tableware tools for cutting and eating food.

B. Manners behaved while eating.

C. Manners kept by those who work with knives, forks and spoons.

D. Tableware for guests to use at the table.

(5) What can we learn from this program?

A. People often feel worried when they use forks.

B. People can't remember which fork should be used first.

C. It's no need to worry when you take a wrong fork.

D. It's common to use the forks from outside in.

Task 3

 Now listen to the program twice and complete the dictation task by filling in the blanks numbered 1 to 6 with the exact words. At the end of this task, there will be a pause for you to check what you've written.

Alright, Jonathan (1) _____ taking the lead from your host or (2) _____. And Liz (3) _____ a few basic table manner (4) _____. First, don't eat with your mouth open. Like this (making noise). And that's (5) _____ very rude. Second rule, don't put your (6) _____ on the table.

IV   Additional Listening Material

Directions: *In this part, you are going to listen to a program. When you listen to this program for the first time, you should pay attention to its main ideas and answer some general comprehension questions. When you listen for the second time, you should focus on important details and answer some specific comprehension questions. When the program is repeated for the third time, you should complete the dictation task.*

Glossary

(1) pram *n.* 婴儿车	(4) offend *v.* 冒犯
(2) pushchair *n.* 婴儿车	(5) admiration *n.* 敬意/佩服
(3) courtesy *n.* 礼貌	

Task 1

Now listen to the program for the first time and answer questions 1 to 2.

(1) What is the program mainly about?

    A. Information of the city transportation.

    B. Various ways of communication.

    C. Good British manners.

    D. Convenience of making a telephone.

(2) What are the five foreigners talking about?

    A. How British people behave in public places.

    B. How people react to the good manners.

    C. Who should be treated politely.

    D. Who should be polite to others.

Task 2

Now listen to the program for the second time and answer questions 3 to 5.

(3) What does "courtesy" mean?

    A. Respectful or considerate act.

    B. An assembly to conduct judicial business.

    C. Education imparted in a series of lessons or meetings.

    D. Tableware implements for cutting and eating food.

(4) Who should a seat be given up for according to the program?

    A. A serious ill patient.   B. People at the age of about 50.

    C. Women with children.   D. People with luggage.

(5) How do British people use their mobile phones?

    A. Turn it on anytime and anywhere.

    B. Answer the phone in a haste impatiently.

    C. Power off in the meetings or conferences.

    D. Pick it up and answer loudly in a restaurant.

Task 3

Now listen to the program twice and complete the dictation task by filling in the blanks numbered 1 to 6 with the exact words or sentences with exact words. At the end of this task, there will be a pause for you to check what you've written.

British people are very polite in the way they talk. They are just so lovely. They use a lot of (1) _____ like please and thank you and excuse me and (2) _____ of sentences are (3) _____ polite. Even in the situation when there is a lot of (4) _____ in the air they would be talking to you in a very very polite manner and they would make sure that the (5) _____ is on a very very polite level and nobody gets (6) _____ with the way they speak to them.

V Video-aural Material

Directions: *In this part, you are going to watch a video clip. When you watch the video for the first time, you should pay attention to its main ideas and answer some general comprehension questions. When the clip is played for the second time, you should focus on important details and answer some specific comprehension questions. When the clip is repeated for the third and fourth time, you should complete the sentences with the words or phrases you have heard in the news.*

Task 1

Now watch the video for the first time and answer questions 1 to 2.

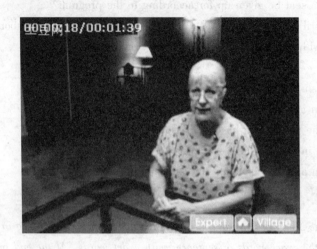

(1) What does this clip tell us?

  A. Children's behavior.

  B. Children's games.

  C. Children's favorite in a restaurant.

  D. Children's proper dining manner.

(2) What is the old lady?

  A. A host in a TV station.   B. A host for a website.

  C. A manager in a restaurant.   D. A teacher of a nursery.

Task 2

👁 *Now watch the clip for the second time and answer questions 3 to 5.*

(3) What does the word "specials" mean?

  A. A meal with specific feature and flavor.

  B. An important requirement in a restaurant.

  C. An extra service in a restaurant.

  D. A manner used especially in a restaurant.

(4) What is the meaning for "excuse" in this clip?

  A. Express forgiveness.

  B. Give his own proper reasons.

  C. Say farewell politely.

D. Take one's own responsibility.

(5) What is the good manner when finishing a dinner in a restaurant?

    A. To show your fullness.

    B. To express your appreciation.

    C. Just to say goodbye.

    D. Just to pay the bill.

Task 3

👀 *Now watch the video twice and complete the sentences by filling in the blanks numbered* 1 *to* 7 *with the words and phrases you have just heard in the clip. At the end of this task, there will be a pause for you to check what you've written.*

When you're at the restaurant and the waiter comes to your order, you should (1) _____ say "May I please have this" or you can ask "Could you please tell me some of your (2) _____" and with your children too teaching them proper manners of the table, saying please and thank you when they've been (3) _____ something or ask for something. Also when they have (4) _____ their meal, they should ask to be (5) _____ that they finished, and they might (6) _____ that the meal was (7) _____.

<table>
<tr><td>VI</td><td></td></tr>
</table>

Listening Skills

1. The skills of short conversations (2)

In choosing the right answer to the question after listening to a conversation, we have found there are two kinds of questions designed for the short conversation, i. e. questions for direct choice or indirect choice. If you're familiar with the basic rules in designing questions, they will help you understand the right answer.

(1) Direct choice

Direct choice is a kind of design which gives students a hint or a match to get the correct answer, because the word, or the phrase or the sentence in the conversation is quite similar or even the same to one of the four choices. For example:

W: Excuse me, I am a stranger here. Can you tell me the way to the railway station?

M: OK. Go straight and turn left. You can't miss it.

Q: Why does the woman ask the way?

    A. Because she is old enough.

    B. Because she is ill.

    C. Because it is the first time for her to be here.

    D. Because it is very difficult for her to go home by herself.

Here, "it is the first time for her to be here" is quite similar in meaning to "I am a stranger". By way of direct choice, item C is sure to be the key to the question.

(2) Indirect choice

Indirect choice means that the key is implied between the lines. It is not easy to get the key on the surface meaning of the conversation. For example:

W: My darling. Today is Sunday.

M: Yes. But I have to leave now.

Q: What does the woman mean?

    A. She wants to help her husband go out for business.

    B. She wants to ask her husband to do housework instead.

    C. She wants to cook good dishes for her husband.

    D. She wants to sweep the floor with her husband.

From this conversation, we can judge from her tone of voice that she wants to have a rest on Sunday. She wishes her husband could stay at home doing housework instead. So B is the correct answer. However, we can not find such words from its surface meaning. We should catch the meaning according to the content and the tone of voice.

2. Sample practice

Directions: *In this section you will hear* 10 *short conversations. At the end of each conversation a question will be asked about what was said. Both the conversation and the question will be spoken only once. After each question there will be a pause. During the pause you must read the four choices marked A, B, C and D, and decide which is the best answer.* 🔊

(1) A. Get some change from Lucy.
    B. Go to look for a bus.
    C. Use the woman's car.
    D. Pay for the bus.

(2) A. At school.
    B. In the classroom.
    C. At a bookstore.
    D. In a library.

(3) A. She will help the man to catch up.
    B. She is worried about the man's health.
    C. She looked after him when he was in hospital.
    D. She's bought the man a pair of glasses today.

(4) A. He is going to drink too much with her father.
    B. He is eager to meet Susan's parents.
    C. He has the same hobby as Susan's father.
    D. He thinks drinking is a good way to kill time.

(5) A. He finds the presentation hard to follow.
    B. He speaks highly of the presentation.
    C. He considers the presentation very dull.
    D. He thinks Professor White has chosen an interesting topic.

(6) A. A small bookshelf.
    B. A second-hand typewriter.
    C. Some useful stocks.
    D. High quality paper.

(7) A. They set off early.

B. They wait for a fine day.

C. They go sightseeing.

D. They go to the seaside.

(8) A. He likes to show off in class.

B. He is a good student.

C. He has a funny face.

D. He is a handsome guy.

(9) A. Her car can stand any crash.

B. Her car is kept in bad condition.

C. Her car is not as good as his.

D. Her car is maintained as well as his.

(10) A. She is too busy to go.

B. She's willing to go shopping.

C. She doesn't want to wait long.

D. She enjoys the beautiful weather.

3. Additional training

Directions: *In this section, you will hear 10 short conversations. At the end of each conversation, a question will be asked about what was said. Both the conversation and the question will be spoken only once. After each question there will be a pause. During the pause, you must read the four choices marked A, B, C and D, and decide which is the best answer.*

(1) A. His father.   B. His mother.

C. His brother.   D. His sister.

(2) A. A job opportunity.

B. A position as general manager.

C. A big travel agency.

D. An inexperienced salesman.

(3) A. Having a rest.

   B. Continuing the meeting.

   C. Moving on to the next item.

   D. Waiting a little longer.

(4) A. The weather forecast says it will be fine.

   B. The weather doesn't count in their plan.

   C. They will do as planned in case of rain.

   D. They will postpone their program if it rains.

(5) A. He finds it necessary to choose another course.

   B. He finds it hard to follow the teacher.

   C. He doesn't like the teacher because he talks more.

   D. He doesn't like the teacher's accent.

(6) A. Go on with the game.

   B. Review his lessons.

   C. Draw pictures on the computer.

   D. Have a good rest.

(7) A. She does not agree with the man.

   B. The man's performance is disappointing.

   C. Most people will find basketball boring.

   D. She shares the man's opinion.

(8) A. The man went to a wrong gate.

   B. The man has just missed his flight.

   C. The plane will leave at 9:14.

   D. The plane's departure time remains unknown.

(9) A. At a newsstand.

   B. At a car dealer's.

   C. At a publishing house.

   D. At a newspaper office.

(10) A. He wants to get a new position.
  B. He is asking the woman for help.
  C. He has left the woman a good impression.
  D. He enjoys letter writing.

I

Preview Exercises

1. Dictation:

Directions: *Watch the video and fill in the blanks.*

"By day I've sold (1) _____. My dream is to spend my life doing what I feel I was born to do..."

"Paul, what are you here for today, Paul?"

"To sing (2) _____."

"I've always wanted to sing as a (3) _____. Confidence's always been sort of like a difficult thing for me. I always find a little bit difficult to be completely (4) _____ in myself."

"Okay, ready when you are."

2. Questions:

(1) What is your first impression of this man and do you think he is excellent when you have the first sight of him?

_____

_____

_____

_____

_____

(2) How do you think of his singing? Do you get any inspiration from him?

_____

_____

_____

_____

_____

_____

Warming up Exercises

1. Background knowledge

What is confidence? What is the correct attitude toward confidence?

Confidence is a kind of feeling that you think you are capable of doing something successfully. It can make you optimistic and pleased. It may be a plus for you to enjoy doing things and enjoy your life. But confidence does not mean you are better than others in whatever aspects or wherever places, that is not confidence but craziness, which might bring a terrible hazard to the human society as well as to oneself.

As we all know, confidence is closely related to one's success. So many people tend to be very confident of themselves. But, sometimes too much confidence or blind confidence would lead you astray. If you want to be successful, the first thing you should do is to be confident of yourself by analyzing your strength and weakness respectively. Then you should know how to overcome your shortcomings by such ways as reasonable analysis, exposure to your friends to seek help, learning from or receiving others' merits so as to make yourself even more confident. Are there any other ways to make you confident? Surely, there are. You can get to them through the listening practice.

2. Questions

Do you think you are special or you have the talent which other people do not possess?

3. Check the preview exercises

Listening Material

Directions: *In this part, you are going to listen to a report. When you listen to the report for the first time, you should pay attention to its main ideas and answer some general comprehension questions. When you listen to it for the second time, you should fo-*

cus on important details and answer some specific comprehension questions. When part of the report is repeated for the third and fourth time, you should complete the dictation task.

Task 1

🔊 *Now listen to the report for the first time and answer questions 1 to 2.*

(1) What is the purpose of the report?

　　A. To teach us how to dress.

　　B. To teach us how to speak up.

　　C. To teach us how to know ourselves.

　　D. To teach us how to be confident.

(2) Which of the followings is not mentioned by the speaker?

　　A. To speak up.

　　B. To dress well.

　　C. To make up.

　　D. To compliment others.

Task 2

🔊 *Now listen to the report for the second time and answer questions 3 to 5.*

(3) When will you look taller?

　　A. Dressing well.

　　B. With better posture.

　　C. Walking faster.

　　D. With a big smile.

(4) What is the merit of complimenting others?

　　A. To help others know themselves better.

　　B. To help you know others better.

　　C. To help break the cycle of negativity.

　　D. Help you know others better.

(5) What will walking 25% faster result in?

　　A. Changing your character and temperament.

B. Making you look and feel more important.

C. Finding your best performance in yourself.

D. Helping you look and feel much healthier.

🔊 *Now listen to part of the report twice and complete the dictation task by filling in the blanks numbered 1 to 10 with the exact words or sentences, or with the main points in your own words.*

1. When you (1) _____, you feel better and (2) _____ your self-confidence.

2. People with (3) _____ walk quickly. They have (4) _____ work to do and they don't have all day to do it.

3. By practicing good (5) _____, you'll notice how much more confident you feel. With better posture, you'll be (6) _____ taller.

4. Help break this cycle of (7) _____. Steer clear of (8) _____ and make an effort to compliment other people.

5. Make an effort to speak up at least once in every group (9) _____. When you can (10) _____.

IV Additional Listening Material

Directions: *In this part, you are going to listen to a report. When you listen to the report for the first and second time, you should pay attention to its main idea and answer some general comprehension questions. When part of the report is repeated for the third and the fourth time, you should complete the dictation task.*

Glossary

(1) Sufiya Abdur-Rahman *n.* （人名）	(4) ethnic *adj.* 种族的
(2) sibling *n.* 兄弟姐妹	(5) apparently *adv.* 显然地
(3) resume *n.* 简历	(6) out of the question 不可能

Now listen to the report for the first time and answer questions 1 to 2.

(1) How are the blacks treated in the United States according to the speaker?

    A. Equal.

    B. Unequal.

    C. Ignored.

    D. Highlighted.

(2) How does the speaker feel being a black?

    A. Indifferent.

    B. Proud.

    C. Inferior.

    D. Superior.

Now listen to the report for the second time and answer questions 3 to 5.

(3) What is the girl's problem?

    A. She finds it is difficult to spell her name.

    B. People think it is difficult to pronounce her name.

    C. It is very difficult to find a job because of her ethnicity.

    D. Her brother asks to change her name, but she thinks it is no necessary.

(4) What are the achievements made by the black people according to the speaker?

    A. The black music and culture have worldwide impact.

    B. Her elders survived through the hard time.

    C. Her ancestors fought for the equal rights.

    D. Black people are very individual.

(5) What will the speaker do in the future?

    A. To change her name.

    B. To fight for equal rights for black people.

    C. To keep herself being black whenever she goes.

    D. To promote the black culture and traditions worldwide.

🔊 *Now listen to part of the report twice and complete the dictation task by filling in the blanks numbered 1 to 5 with the exact words.*

I love that my African people were among the most individual in the world and I'm constantly amazed that my (1)_____ survived a period of (2)_____ hardship and forever (3)_____ to my grandparents fight for equal (4)_____ and equally admire my brothers for (5)_____ a music and culture with impact worldwide.

V Video-aural Material

Directions: *In this part, you are going to watch a video clip. When you watch the video for the first time, you should pay attention to its main idea and answer some general comprehension questions. When it is played for the second and the third and fourth time, you should complete the sentences with the words or phrases you have just watched.*

Task 1

👁 *Now watch the video for the first time and answer questions 1 to 2.*

(1) How can you learn to love yourself according to the clip?

A. Love others.

B. Give yourself a big hug everyday.

C. Buy yourself a gift.

D. Have big dinner when you are sad.

(2) Why should we listen to ourselves?

A. We are seldom wrong.

B. Nobody knows us better than we know ourselves.

C. Nobody could point out our mistakes except ourselves.

D. We could improve our character from listening to ourselves.

Task 2

👁 *Now watch the video for the second time and answer questions* 3 *to* 5.

(3) According to the video, what can make you feel good?

A. To have a drink.

B. To swim in a pool regularly.

C. To do some volunteer work.

D. To go shopping with your friends.

(4) What does the word "*garbage*" mean in the sentence "Too often we dump a lot of garbage... "?

A. Food that is discarded.

B. A worthless message.

C. A container where waste can be discarded.

D. A case used to carry belongings when traveling.

(5) How can you get rid of the negatives according to the video?

A. To play sports.

B. To talk and explain to your friends.

C. To listen to some music.

D. To have a drink.

Task 3

👁 *Now watch the video twice and complete the sentences by filling in the blanks numbered* 1 *to 7 with the words and phrases you have just watched. At the end of this task, there will be a pause for you to check what you've written.*

The first one you can do is (1) _____. Now this takes a bit of practice and looks kind of funny, but try, it'll work for you.

Now the second technique: (2) _____. So every time you pass a mirror, look into it and (3) _____.

But the third thing: (4) _____ and that can be anything from listening to some music, taking hikes, doing volunteer work or even just taking a bath.

Now the fourth thing: (5) _____. Nobody knows you better than you know yourself.

The fifth thing: (6) _____. Yeah, not like you're crazy or something like that, but in times of stress, take a timeout break.

So the sixth thing is to (7) _____. If anything feels like it's dragging you down, get rid of it.

VI Listening Skills

1. The listening skills of long conversation

Long conversation is a very important item in listening comprehension. It is a conversation with several rounds happened between two speakers, followed by 3 or 4 questions. Students may feel difficult to grasp so much information in such a short time. Therefore, mastering proper listening skills can help you much to reduce the unnecessary loss.

(1) To focus on the beginning, the middle and the end of the conversation. Questions are usually attached to these parts.

(2) To scan the questions or choices before your listening, you can guess the possible listening contents or exclude the choices which are obviously wrong according to your common

sense or understanding of this topic.

(3) To take notes while listening, especially some important details, e. g. numbers, synonyms and signal words, such as: that is, however, put it into another way, etc.

(4) To predict their utterance during your listening with the help of signal words, such as because, therefore, first, second, etc.

(5) To prepare yourself before listening with vocabulary related to college life, study, work, recreation, etc.

2. **Sample practice**

Questions 1 to 4 are based on the conversation you have just heard.

---

(1) install   *v.* 安装
(2) range from   从……到……变动
(3) all the way up to   直至
(4) What's the picture?   情况怎样?
(5) aggressive   *adj.* 好斗的,攻击性的
(6) justify   *v.* 替……辩护,证明,证明正当
(7) look into   调查,观察
(8) draw up   拟定(起草,拉起,画出)
(9) index   *n.* 索引
(10) reference desk   参考咨询台
(11) Periodical Literature 期刊文献

---

(1) What are the two speakers talking about?

    A. The benefits of strong business competition.

    B. A proposal to lower the cost of production.

    C. Complaints about the expense of modernization.

    D. Suggestions concerning new business strategies.

(2) What does the woman say about the equipment for their factory?

    A. It costs much more than its worth.

    B. It should be brought up to date.

    C. It calls for immediate repairs.

    D. It can still be used for a long time.

(3) What does the woman suggest about human resources?

    A. The personnel manager should be fired for inefficiency.

B. A few engineers should be employed to modernize the factory.

C. The entire staff should be retrained.

D. Better-educated employees should be promoted.

(4) Why does the woman suggest advertising on TV?

A. Their competitors have long been advertising on TV.

B. TV commercials are less expensive.

C. Advertising in newspapers alone is not sufficient.

D. TV commercials attract more investments.

3. Additional training

Questions 1 to 3 are based on the conversation you have just heard.

(1) What is the man doing?

A. Searching for reference material.

B. Watching a film of the 1930s'.

C. Writing a course book.

D. Looking for a job in a movie studio.

(2) What does the librarian think of the topic the man is working on?

A. It's too broad to cope with.

B. It's a bit outdated.

C. It's controversial.

D. It's of little practical value.

(3) Where can the man find the relevant magazine articles?

A. At the end of the online catalogue.

B. At the Reference Desk.

C. In the New York Times.

D. In the Reader's Guide to Periodical Literature.

Unit Four Gratitude

Preview Exercises

1. Dictation:

Directions: *Listen and dictate what you've heard.*

_____

_____

_____

_____

_____

2. Questions:

(1) What difficulties did Chinese meet in the year of 2008?

_____

_____

_____

_____

(2) How do Chinese people react when they suffered the difficulties?

_____

_____

_____

_____

II

Warming up Exercises

Background knowledge

1. A brief introduction to gratitude
    (1) The reasons why we have gratitude.
    (2) The ways we express our gratitude.
2. Check the preview exercises

Listening Material

Directions: *In this part, you are going to listen to a report. When you listen to the report for the first time, you should pay attention to its main ideas and answer some general comprehension questions. When you listen to it for the second time, you should focus on important details and answer some specific comprehension questions. When part of the report is repeated for the third and fourth time, you should complete the dictation task.*

Glossary

(1) dime *n.* 硬币	(4) baffled *v.* 困惑,为难
(2) owe *v.* 亏欠	(5) gown *n.* 长外衣,袍子
(3) critically *adv.* 严重地	

Task 1

◀ *Now listen to the material for the first time and answer questions 1 to 2.*

(1) What is true based on the passage?

    A. The doctor was actually the young boy who accepted the help from the girl.

    B. The girl asked help from the doctor Howard Kelly.

    C. The girl paid her bill by a glass of milk.

    D. The boy is looking for the girl.

(2) What can we infer from the passage?

    A. The girl did not believe in God until someone nameless helped her to pay the bill.

    B. The girl's parents stopped to support the boy after two month.

    C. The girl has died at the end because of critical illness.

    D. The boy has been grateful to her help all his life.

Task 2

◀ *Now listen to the material for the second time and answer questions 3 to 5.*

(3) What did the doctor Howard Kelly write on her bill?

    A. "Paid in full with a glass of milk."

B. "A glass of milk."

C. "Thank you."

D. "How much do I owe you?"

(4) What did the boy do when he felt hungry and cold?

A. Asking for help door by door.

B. Taking some pictures.

C. Selling goods.

D. Looking for his money.

(5) What did the girl give to the boy?

A. A glass of water.

B. A glass of milk.

C. A cake.

D. A bill note.

Task 3

🔊 *Now listen to the material twice and complete the dictation task by filling in the blanks numbered* 1 *to* 10 *with the words, phrases or sentences.*

One day, a poor boy who was trying to pay his way through school by selling goods door to door found that he only had one dime left. He was hungry so he decided to beg for a meal at the next house.

However, he lost his (1) _____ when a lovely young woman opened the door. Instead of a meal he asked for a drink of water. She thought he looked hungry so she brought him a large glass of milk. He drank it slowly, and then asked, "How much do I (2) _____ you?"

"You don't owe me anything," she (3) _____. "Mother has taught me never to accept pay for a kindness." He said, "Then I thank you from the (4) _____ of my heart." As Howard Kelly left that house, he not only felt (5) _____, but it also increased his faith in God and the human race. He was about to give up and quit before this point.

Years later the young woman became (6) _____ ill. The local doctors were baffled.

They finally sent her to the big city, where (7) _____ can be called in to study her rare disease. Dr. Howard Kelly, now famous was called in for the (8) _____. When he heard the name of the town she came from, a strange light filled his eyes. Immediately, he rose and went down through the hospital hall into her room.

Dressed in his doctor's gown he went in to see her. He recognized her at once. He went back to the consultation room and (9) _____ to do his best to save her life. From that day on, he gave special attention to her case.

After a long struggle, the battle was won. (10) _____. He looked at it and then wrote something on the side. The bill was sent to her room. She was afraid to open it because she was positive that it would take the rest of her life to pay it off. Finally she looked, and the note on the side of the bill caught her attention. She read these words...

"Paid in full with a glass of milk."

Tears of joy flooded her eyes as she prayed silently: "Thank You, God. Your love has spread through human hearts and hands."

IV   Additional Listening Material

Directions: *In this part, you are going to listen to a report. When you listen to it for the first time, you should pay attention to its main idea and answer some general comprehension questions. When you listen to it for the second time, you should focus on important details and answer some specific comprehension questions. When part of the report is repeated for the third and the fourth time, you should complete the dictation task.*

Glossary

(1) lethargy *n.* 懒散	(3) conscious *adj.* 有意识的, 清楚的
(2) impairment *n.* 损伤, 破坏	(4) listless *adj.* 无精打采的

Task 1

Now listen to the report for the first time and answer questions 1 to 2.

(1) What does this passage tell us?

    A. Death of human being.

    B. How do blind people survive?

    C. Cherishing what we have.

    D. Findings in a forest.

(2) What do we learn from the passage?

    A. Life is so important that each of us must cherish it.

    B. Blind people always find something special in lives.

    C. The author's friend cannot talk.

    D. People always have listless attitude towards life when they are in health.

Task 2

Now listen to the report for the second time and answer questions 3 to 5.

(3) Why does the author mention the examples of faculties and senses?

    A. To show the function of hearing and seeing.

    B. To explain in details about how to make good use of human's faculties.

    C. To criticize those who are hardly aware of listless attitude towards life.

    D. To express the manifold bleesing given by god.

(4) What is the author's attitude towards people who can see and hear?

    A. The author blamed them because they don't make good use of their faculties.

    B. The author envies them because they can see and hear what author cannot.

    C. The author disliked them because they take offense to the author.

    D. The author had hatred to them because they ignore what they've heard and seen.

(5) How did the author view when her friend told her there was nothing particular in the forest?

    A. She thought her friend cheated.

    B. She convinced that her friend did not realized what she had seen.

    C. She blamed her because her friend was so careless.

    D. She did not believe what her friend said.

Now listen to the report twice and complete the dictation task by filling in the blanks numbered 1 to 10 with the words or sentence.

Most of us take life for (1) _____. We know that one day we must die, but usually we picture that day as far in the future; when we are in (2) _____ health, death is all but unimaginable. We (3) _____ think of it. The days (4) _____ out in an endless vista. So we go about our petty task, hardly aware of our listless attitude towards life. The same lethargy, I am afraid, (5) _____ the use of our faculties and senses. Only the deaf appreciate hearing, only the blind realize the manifold blessings that lie in sight. Particularly does this observation apply to those who have lost sight and hearing in adult life? But those who have never (6) _____ impairment of sight or hearing seldom make the fullest use of these blessed (7) _____. Their eyes and ears take in all sights and sound hazily, without (8) _____, and with little appreciation. It is the same old story of not being grateful for what we conscious of health until we are ill. I have often thought it would be a blessing if each human being were (9) _____ blind and deaf for a few days at some time during his early adult life. (10) _____. Now and then I have tested my seeing friends to discover what they see. Recently I was visited by a very good friend who had just returned from a long walk in the woods, and I asked her what she had observed. "Nothing in particular," she replied. I might have been incredulous had I not been accustomed to such responses, for long ago I became convinced that the seeing see little.

Video-aural Material

Directions: *In this part, you are going to watch a video clip. When you watch the video for the first time, you should pay attention to its main idea and answer some general comprehension questions. When it is played for the second time, you should focus on important details and answer some specific comprehension questions. When the clip is repeated for the third and fourth time, you should complete the sentences with the words or phrases you have just watched.*

Task 1

Now watch the video for the first time and answer questions 1 to 2.

(1) What lesson does the teacher teach?

    A. English Literature.

    B. Poem Writing.

    C. English Culture.

    D. Rhythm of Poem.

(2) How did the student in the episode complete the task?

    A. Some of them completed the task fully.

    B. None of them completed the task fully.

    C. All of them completed the task partially.

    D. None of them completed the task partially.

Task 2

👁 *You can watch it for the second time and then answer the questions 3 to 5.*

(3) What can we learn from the episode?

    A. All the students are afraid of writing.

    B. A lot of students do not complete the homework.

    C. The teacher is so disappointed when he finds someone does not finish his task.

    D. Todd has talent to write poems.

(4) What kind of personality does Todd has?

    A. Aggressive, independent.

B. Analytical, well-balanced.

C. Self-assured, trustworthy.

D. Romantic, sensitive.

(5) What do we learn about Mr. Keating?

A. He teaches his students with conventional ways.

B. He loves poem writing.

C. He encourages his students a lot.

D. He teaches writing so successfully.

Task 3

 Now watch the video twice and complete the dictation task by filling in the blanks numbered 1 to 10 with the words or sentence.

—Mr. Anderson, I see you (1) _____ there in (2) _____. Come on, Todd, step up. Let's put you (3) _____ your (4) _____.

—I, I didn't do it. I didn't write a (5) _____.

—Mr. Anderson thinks that everything (6) _____ of him is worthless and (7) _____. Isn't that right, Todd? (8) _____ that your (9) _____ fear? Well, I think you're wrong. (10) _____.

| VI | **Listening Skills** |

1. The skills of short passages

Short passage listening comprehension tests the pronunciation, glossaries and grammar in addition to analyzing, reasoning and inferring. Due to the instant of listening, the candidates feel so difficult to understand what they have heard without any aid of written information. However, it does not mean short passage listening has no techniques to follow. The questions for short passages involve catching the main idea, details and inferring as well. Also, short passages concern narration and exposition both. Now, we are taking some examples to display some skills when you do short passage listening comprehension.

(1) Explore the questions and statement both before your listening.

Listening is an extremely complex communicative activity. It is a "temporally extended activity" in which the listener "continuously develops more or less specific readiness for what will come next". In other words, an effective listener is constantly setting up hypothesis in his mind, and also, he is constantly testing his hypothesis by matching it with what he has heard in reality. If he hears what he has expected, he receives the information. But if what he hears is totally out of his expectation, he fails to get the message. So, it is so important to explore the questions and statement both before listening that the candidates have some information for the short passages already.

(2) Pay much attention to "wh-"questions.

Short passage listening is focusing the main idea, detail as well as inference. All these questions could be showed with the ways of "who", "when", "what", "where", "why" and "how". Here are some examples:

What is the main idea of the passage?

What can we learn from this passage?

What is the best title for this passage?

What is the passage mainly about?

What is the speaker most concerned about?

How does the writer feel about...

What can we infer from the passage?

(3) Read more out of your classroom. Short passage listening concerns many types of writing. Also, short passages can talk about culture, society in western countries. It requires candidate to acknowledge more out of their textbooks.

2. Sample practice

(1) What did Joan Higginbotham do before joining in NASA?

    A. She was a tailor.

    B. She was an engineer.

    C. She was an educator.

    D. She was a public speaker.

(2) How does Higginbotham prepare her speech on space walks?

A. Basing them on science-fiction movies.

B. Including interesting examples in them.

C. Adjusting them to different audiences.

D. Focusing on the latest progress in space science.

（3）What does the high school audience want to know about space travel?

A. Whether spacemen carry weapons.

B. How spacesuits protect spacemen.

C. How NASA trains its spacemen.

D. What spacemen cat and drink.

3. Additional training

（1）Why does the speaker say there are great possibilities for communication breakdowns?

A. People differ greatly in their ability to communicate.

B. There are numerous languages in existence.

C. Most public languages are inherently vague.

D. Big gaps exist between private and public languages.

（2）What is Chomsky's point on the ability to learn a language?

A. It is a sign of human intelligence.

B. It improves with constant practice.

C. It is something we are born with.

D. It varies from person to person.

（3）What does Chomsky's theory fail to explain according to the speaker?

A. How private languages are developed.

B. How different languages are related.

C. How people create their languages.

D. How children learn to use language.

Unit Five College Life

Preview Exercises

1. Dictation:

Directions: *Listen and dictate what you've heard.*

🔊 _____

_____

_____

_____

2. Questions:

(1) What's the difference between *college* and *university*?

_____

_____

_____

_____

(2) What does *institute* refer to?

_____

_____

_____

_____

Warming up Exercises

Background knowledge

1. A brief introduction to college life

(1) College facilities (residence hall, college cafeteria, college library).

(2) Phrases about university activities.

(3) Dissertation.

(4) Going abroad for further study.

(5) Successful language learner.

2. Check the preview exercises

III Listening Material

Directions: *In this part, you are going to listen to a report. When you listen to the report for the first time, you should pay attention to its main ideas and answer some general comprehension questions. When you listen to it for the second time, you should focus on important details and answer some specific comprehension questions. When the report is repeated for the third and the fourth time, you should complete the dictation task.*

Task 1

◁ *Now listen to the report for the first time and answer questions 1 to 2.*

(1) Which of the following statement is true ?

    A. A graduate can be a person either got a master's degree or a doctorate.

    B. People can get a PhD while he is working with a full time job.

    C. More than 34,000 students received a research doctorate in 2005.

    D. Immigrants from China, South Korea, India, Taiwan etc. got one-third of the doctorates in the USA.

(2) What should people do in order to get a doctor's degree according to the report?

    A. To take special IQ tests.

    B. To carry out original research.

    C. To present their findings by publishing a book.

    D. To ask a group of people to defend them.

Task 2

◁ *Now listen to the report for the second time and answer questions 3 to 5.*

(3) Students who major in _____ receive a BA degree.

    A. Mechanical Engineering

    B. Genetics

    C. Computer Science and Technology

    D. Journalism

(4) After students have a _____ degree, they may go on to earn a _____ degree.

A. graduate,   master's

B. undergraduate,   bachelor's

C. bachelor's,   graduate

D. doctor's,   graduate

(5) Someone with a PhD is a "doctor of philosophy". It means _____.

A. He must be a philosopher who is majoring in philosophy.

B. He may major in philosophy or education.

C. He must be a doctor working in hospital.

D. He must be a graduate and has already got master's degree.

Task 3

Now listen to the report twice and complete the dictation task by filling in the blanks numbered 1 to 8 with the exact words or sentences, or with the main points in your own words. At the end of this task, there will be a pause for you to check what you've written.

Students can receive a PhD in (1) _____, social work, education, music, history and a lot of other areas. Requirements can (2) _____ one university to another, and from one area of study to another. But the National Science Foundation says American doctoral education is organized around a research experience.

A PhD usually requires at least 3 years of (3) _____ study after a bachelor's degree. Some people first get a master's degree, other do not. PhD (4) _____ must also pass special examinations and carry out original research. Students present their findings by writing a dissenrtation, a long paper that they have to defend before a group of (5) _____.

Every year, the (6) _____ government collects information on research doctorates awarded in the United States. More than 43000 students received a research doctorate in 2005, the most recent year reported. Close to one-third of those doctorates went to foreign students in the United States on a (7) _____ visa.

(8) _____

The University of Illinois awarded the largest number of doctorates to foreign students. The other universities in the top five were Purdue, Ohio State, Texas A&M and Pennsylvania State.

Ⅳ Additional Listening Material

Directions: *In this part, you are going to listen to a report. When you listen to the report for the first time, you should pay attention to its main ideas and answer some general comprehension questions. When you listen to it for the second time, you should focus on important details and answer some specific comprehension questions. When the report is repeated for the third and the fourth time, you should complete the dictation task.*

Glossary

(1) division *n.* (机构的)部门	(4) commonwealth *n.* 州
(2) constitution *n.* 宪法,章程	(5) charity *n.* 慈善机构(或组织)
(3) Pennsylvania *n.* 宾夕法尼亚州	(6) Philadelphia *n.* 费城

Task 1

Now listen to the report for the first time and answer questions 1 to 2.

(1) What is your understanding of higher education in America according to the report?

A. More than 4200 2-year schools award degrees in the United States.

B. Students can get higher education in Harvard than any other universities.

C. About two fifth of Harvard students are from other countries.

D. University of Pennsylvania and Havard University are both old institutions of higher learning.

(2) Which following statement about Harvard University is true？

A. Harvard University includes Harvard College, Radcliff College, and ten other schools.

    B. Harvard University is a graduate school.

    C. Harvard University began in 1636 in Cambridge, Massachusetts.

    D. Harvard University was officially recognized as a university in 1718.

Task 2

🔊 *Now listen to the report for the second time and answer questions 3 to 5.*

(3) How was Harvard University like when it was established originally?

    A. It had several bookstores on the campus.

    B. It had one lecturer and nine students.

    C. It had students from all over the world.

    D. It had faculty members teaching a variety of subjects.

(4) Harvard University got its name because of _____.

    A. it's location at Harvard, Massachusetts.

    B. a puritan named Harvard.

    C. a student named John Harvard.

    D. a rich book seller named Harvard.

(5) The reasons why University of Pennsylvania considers itself as America's oldest university are as follows except that _____.

    A. University of Pennsylvania was established in 1751.

    B. the Charity School of Philadelphia, the forerunner of University of Pennsylvania, was established in 1740.

    C. the Commonwealth of Pennsylvania recognized University of Pennsylvania as a university in 1779.

    D. University of Pennsylvania was recognized as a university one year earlier than Harvard University.

Task 3

🔊 *Now listen to the report twice and complete the dictation task by filling in the blanks numbered 1 to 8 with the exact words or sentences, or with the main points in your own words. At the end of this task, there will be a pause for you to check what you've written.*

There are 14 schools at Harvard. They (1) _____ Harvard College and the Radcliff

Institute for Advanced Study. Harvard College is the undergraduate (2) _____ of the university and Radcliff is a former college for (3) _____. So Harvard came first. Later, in 1780, the Massachusetts (4) _____ went into effect and officially recognized Harvard as a university. Some Harvard materials call it America's oldest university.

But the University of Pennsylvania calls itself America's oldest university. Penn officials (5) _____ that the Commonwealth of Pennsylvania recognized their school as a university in 1779. That was one year before Harvard.

Yet the history gets a little (6) _____. Penn considers its (7) _____ date to be 1740. That was when the Charity School of Philadelphia was established, though it never opened. Benjamin Franklin later (8) _____ his ideas for a learning institution that included the Charity School. It opened in 1751 and became the university.

Ⅴ　Video-aural Material

Directions: *In this part, you are going to watch a video clip. When you watch the video for the first time, you should pay attention to its main idea and answer some general comprehension questions. When it is played for the second time, you should focus on important details and answer some specific comprehension questions. When the clip is repeated for the third and fourth time, you should complete the sentences with the words or phrases you have just watched.*

Glossary

(1) residency　*n.* 医生的实习期	(6) limb　*n.* 肢体
(2) thrill　*n.* 激动	(7) phantom　*n.* 幻觉
(3) zygote　*n.* 受精卵	(8) sorrow　*n.* 悲伤
(4) embrace　*v.* 拥抱	(9) anticipation　*n.* 期待
(5) victim　*n.* 遇难者	(10) dread　*n.* 不安

Task 1

☞ *Now watch the video for the first time and answer questions 1 to 2.*

(1) The scene of the episode was on _____.

    A. high school graduation.

    B. college graduation.

    C. the homecoming.

    D. adult ceremony.

(2) On the playground what did the girl ask her classmate to do?

    A. To write down his telephone number.

    B. To paint a portrait.

    C. To look at Johnson's signature.

    D. To sigh his name on the year book.

Task 2

👁 *Now watch the video for the second time and answer questions 3 to 5.*

(3) What personality do you think the girl has?

    A. Ill-tempered.

    B. Quiet.

    C. Quick-tempered.

    D. Cheerful.

(4) How did the girl feel when she graduated from high school?

    A. Joy.

B. Sorrow.

C. Dread.

D. Anticipation.

(5) Where do you think the girl will go for college study?

A. Stanford.

B. New York city.

C. Washington.

D. Harvard.

Task 3

👁 *Now watch the video twice and complete the sentences by filling in the blanks numbered* 1 *to* 20 *with the words and phrases you have just watched. At the end of this task, there will be a pause for you to check what you've written.*

Dear Sally, you should probably be (1) _____ for this. First of all, everything was (2) _____.

I mean, in three months, I'd be at Stanford (3) _____; then I'd start my four years (4) _____ at one of the Stanford (5) _____. My dad was (6) _____.

So on this day, undoubtedly the most (7) _____ of your lives. I urge you to savor the (8) _____, embrace life because these... days will not come again.

It's (9) _____. Sometimes it's the smallest (10) _____ that can (11) _____ much change your life (12) _____. I never said that.

I've (13) _____ you for four years, always (14) _____ what you were like, what was going in on your mind, all the time that you were so (15) _____, just thinking, (16) _____ in your notebook.

I should have just asked you, but I never asked you. So, now, four years later, I don't even (17) _____you, but I (18) _____you.

Well, this makes me sound (19) _____ , but I'm okay with that. So take care of yourself. Love, Ben, P. S. I would have said (20) _____ , but unfortunately we never were in touch.

1. The skills of compound dictation

(1) Compound dictation in CET4

The fourth section of CET4 listening is compound dictation which requires students to listen to a passage for three times and then write down eight missing words and three sentences. Students should fill in the eight missing words with the exact words they hear and fill in the information in three blanks either using the exact words they hear or the main points in their own words.

(2) Skills

① Scan the passage for the main ideas while the direction in Compound Dictation is being read. Predict and make guess what word could be used and what is expected to be talked about in the last three blanks.

② For the first time listening, write down first few letters of the missing words of first eight blanks. Then focus on understanding the meaning of last three sentences. Do not try to write down every word and just write down a few key words of a sentence first, such as subject, verb, object, and conjunction.

③ For the second time listening, complete the first eight blanks quickly and write down more words of last three sentences. Pay special attention to the sentence structure and transitional words such as therefore, while, however, who, etc. The sentences tested are usually parallel sentences and compound sentences.

④ For the third time listening, try to complete the words and sentences.

2. Sample practice

Directions: *In this section, you will hear a passage three times. When the passage is read for the first time, you should listen carefully for its general idea. When the passage is read for the second time, you are required to fill in the blanks from 1 to 8 with the exact words you have just heard. For blanks numbered from 9 to 11 you are required to fill in the missing information. For these blanks, you can either use the exact words you have just heard or write down the main points in your own words. Finally, when the passage is read for the third time, you should check what you have written.* ◁∅

Most American colleges and universities accept one or both of the two major tests. One is the Test of English as a Foreign Language, known as the TOEFL. The other is the International English Language Testing System, or IELTS. The TOEFL is given in 180 countries. The (1)_____ IELTS is given in 121 countries. 1000000 people each year take the TOEFL, says Tom Ewing, a (2)_____ for the Educational Testing Service. Same with the IELTS, says Beryl Meiron, the (3) _____ director of IELTS International. She says 2000 colleges and universities in the United States now (4)_____ the IELTS. Schools might accept it only for undergraduate or graduate (5)_____ , or both. The IELTS is a paper test, while the TOEFL is given on paper only in places where a computer test is (6)__ _____ .

The TOEFL paper test costs $150. It tests reading, listening and writing. A (7) _____ Test of Spoken English costs $125. The computer (8) _____ is called the TOEFL IBT, or Internet-based test. The price is different in each country, but generally falls between $150 and $200. (9) _____ _____ . But with the IELTS, the speaking test is done separately as a live interview. (10) _____ _____ . Everyone takes the same speaking and listening tests. But there is a choice of two kinds of reading and writing tests-either academic or general training. (11)_____ _____ _____ . Institutions in Britain and Australia jointly developed it.

3. Additional training

Directions: *In this section, you will hear a passage three times. When the passage is read for the first time, you should listen carefully for its general idea. When the passage is read for the second time, you are required to fill in the blanks from 1 to 8 with the exact words you have just heard. For blanks numbered from 9 to 11 you are required to fill in the missing information. For these blanks, you can either use the exact words you have just heard or write down the main points in your own words. Finally, when the passage is read for the third time, you should check what you have written.*

Glossary

(1) associate professor 副教授	(6) assistant professor 助理教授
(2) adjunct professor [美]副教授	(7) tenure *n.* 任期/终身教席
(3) academic title 学衔	(8) faculty member 大学教学人员
(4) doctoral degree 博士学位	(9) perish *n.* 死亡,毁灭
(5) instructor *n.* 讲师	(10) candidate *n.* 候选人

Professors usually need a doctorate degree. But, sometimes a school may offer positions to people who have not yet received their doctorate. Such a person would be called an instructor until the degree has been (1) _____. After that, the instructor could become an assistant professor. Assistant professors do not have tenure.

A person with tenure cannot be easily dismissed. Such appointments are permanent. Teachers and (2) _____ who are (3) _____ with the understanding that they will seek tenure are said to be "on the tenure track". Assistant professor is the first job on this (4) _____.

Assistant professors generally have five to (5) _____ years to (6) _____ tenure. During this time, other (7) _____ members study the person's work. If tenure is (8) _____, then the assistant professor usually has a year to find another job.

(9) _____ "Publish or perish" is the traditional saying.

An assistant professor who receives tenure becomes an associate professor. An associate professor may later be appointed as a full professor. Assistant, associate and full professors perform many duties. (10)_____

_____

_____

Other faculty members are not expected to do all these jobs. They are not on a tenure track. Instead, they might be in adjunct or visiting positions. (11)_____

_____

_____

An adjunct professor is also a limited or part-time position, to do research or teach classes. Adjunct professors have a doctorate.

Another position is that of lecturer. Lecturers teach classes, but they may or may not have a doctorate.

Unit Six Networks

I

Preview Exercises

1. Dictation:

Directions: *Listen and dictate what you've heard.*

_____

_____

_____

_____

_____

2. Questions:

(1) List some advantages of networks.

_____

_____

_____

_____

(2) List some disadvantages of networks.

_____

_____

_____

_____

_____

Warming up Exercises

Background knowledge

1. A brief Introduction to networks

(1) Development of networks.

(2) Advantages and disadvantages of networks.

2. Check the preview exercises

III Listening Material

Directions: *In this part, you are going to listen to a report. When you listen to the report for the first time, you should pay attention to its main ideas and answer some general comprehension questions. When you listen to it for the second time, you should focus on important details and answer some specific comprehension questions. When part of the report is repeated for the third and fourth time, you should complete the dictation task.*

Glossary

(1) online   *v.* 在线
(2) attach   *v.* 附加
(3) caffeine   *v.* 咖啡因
(4) virtual   *adj.* 虚幻的
(5) gradually   *adv.* 渐渐地
(6) counseling   *n.* 咨询服务
(7) cranky   *adj.* 任性的,暴躁的
(8) expose   *v.* 曝光

Task 1

◁ *Now listen to the report for the first time and answer questions 1 to 2.*

(1) What is the story talking about?

    A. Addiction to the network.

    B. John's birthday present.

    C. The inconvenience of the network.

    D. The necessity of the Internet.

(2) What can we learn from this story?

    A. Network is both helpful and harmful.

    B. His parents are very angry.

    C. His parents help him to remove his addiction to the network.

    D. Network is the only cause of addicting to the network.

Task 2

◁ *Now listen to the report for the second time and answer questions 3 to 5.*

(3) Why did John's parents take away his computer?

A. Because his computer broke down.

B. Because he did not like to use the computer.

C. Because his parents wanted to use the computer.

D. Because John was suffering from Internet addiction.

(4) What will solve the problem of Internet addiction?

A. Restraining from computer playing.

B. Playing the computer 8 hours a day.

C. Seeking counseling and help.

D. Taking the computer away.

(5) What is not one of the symptoms of Internet addiction?

A. Less connection to the world.

B. Refusing to see others.

C. Crankiness.

D. Gratitude to one's parents.

Task 3

Now listen to the report twice and complete the dictation task by filling in the blanks numbered 1 to 10 with the exact words or sentences either with exact words or its main ideas in your own words. At the end of this task, there will be a pause for you to check what you've written.

On John's (1) _____ birthday, his parents bought him a computer and put it in his room. They thought it would be wise to let him begin learning about the computer and the Internet. When John first started going online, his parents would monitor his online activities. After a (2) _____ period, his parents left him (3) _____.

In a few months they began to notice that John wasn't coming out of his room as often. John liked the Internet, and thought it was a (4) _____ way to connect with virtual friends, and play online games. But as time went on, John became less connected to the real world around him, and more in time with the virtual world that (5) _____ 24 hours a day on the Internet. He became cranky and (6) _____ if his parents asked him to leave the computer. Finally, his parents took away his computer, and (7) _____ counseling for him.

John is not in a class of his own. There are many others who also struggle with what (8) _____ call Internet addiction. Everyone agrees that in this day and age, (9) _____ Thus, access to the Internet can be found in homes, offices, schools, and sometimes even shopping malls. However, the problem of Internet addiction begins when someone is more attached to a virtual online world than the world that exists around them.

(10) _____ Abstaining completely from Internet usage will probably not solve the problem. It is wiser to gradually reduce the amount of time that is spent on the Internet. The Internet can be a wonderful tool that exposes one to many different worlds, but it can also become an addiction, just like caffeine, drugs or smoking. The best way to overcome an addiction is to seek help and counseling if needed.

IV Additional Listening Material

Directions: *In this part, you are going to listen to a piece of news. When you listen to the news for the first time, you should pay attention to its main ideas and answer some general comprehension questions. When you listen to it for the second time, you should focus on important details and answer some specific comprehension questions. When the news is repeated for the third and fourth time, you should complete the dictation task.*

Glossary

(1) linear algebra 线性代数　　　(3) scuba　*n.* 深水呼吸器
(2) anthropology　*n.* 人类学

Task 1

Now listen to the news for the first time and answer questions 1 to 2.

(1) What does this news tell us?

A. Education on the Internet.

B. Free education on the Internet.

C. Introduction to the education of colleges.

D. Introduction to the free education of colleges.

(2) How many schools are mainly involved in this news?

    A. Five.　　　　B. Four.　　　　C. Three.　　　　D. Two.

Task 2

🔊 *Now listen to the news for the second time and answer questions 3 to 5.*

(3) How many subjects can Open Course Ware offer materials from?

    A. 8000.　　　　B. 1800.　　　　C. 1180.　　　　D. 8180.

(4) What can we learn from this news?

A. Now more and more knowledge is on the Internet.

B. Now there is no videos of lectures and demonstrations.

C. Now more students can get credit of degree.

D. Now there are more visitors coming from outside US and Canada.

(5) For what purpose do many visitors often go to the Internet?

A. For finding materials they want.

B. For becoming well known.

C. For self-study.

D. For receiving credit of degree.

Task 3

🔊 *Now listen to the news twice and complete the dictation task by filling in the blanks numbered 1 to 7 with the exact words or sentences with exact words. At the end of this task, there will be a pause for you to check what you've written.*

Today, Open Course Ware (1) _____ materials from one thousand eight hundred (2) _____ and graduate courses. These (3) _____ from physics and linear algebra to anthropology, political science-even scuba diving.

Visitors can learn the same things M. I. T. students learn. But as the site points out, Open-

CourseWare is not an M. I. T. education. Visitors (4) _____ no credit toward a degree. Some materials from a course may not be (5) _____ , and the site does not provide (6) _____ with teachers.

Still, M. I. T. says the (7) _____ has had forty million visits by thirty-one million visitors from almost every country. Sixty percent of the visitors are from outside the United States and Canada.

V   Video-aural Material

Directions: *In this part, you are going to watch a video clip. When you watch the video for the first time, you should pay attention to its main idea and answer some general comprehension questions. When it is played for the second time, you should focus on important details and answer some specific comprehension questions. When the clip is repeated for the third and fourth time, you should complete the sentences with the words or phrases you have just watched.*

Glossary

(1) centigrade *n.* 摄氏	(3) fax *n.* 传真
(2) conference *n.* 会议	(4) update *v.* 更新

👁 *Now watch the video for the first time and answer questions 1 to 2.*

(1) What computer technology make people surprised?

    A. Recognition of human voices.

    B. Control of the growth of plants and vegetables.

    C. Talking through net camera.

    D. Finding everything through searching engines.

(2) What do you know about the central computer?

    A. A computer right in the middle among computers.

    B. A computer controlling the operation of the programs.

    C. A computer whose position is the most important.

    D. A computer used as CPU.

Task 2

👁 *Now watch the video for the second time and answer questions 3 to 5.*

(3) What does "glass house" mean?

    A. A house built with glass.

    B. A house for plants under controlled conditions.

    C. A house producing spectacles.

    D. A house manufacturing glass products.

(4) What can we learn from this article?

    A. Computers can do everything.

    B. Computers play an important role in people's life.

    C. Sound recognition is still in progress.

    D. Searching engines can help us find everything we need.

(5) Which of the following is not true?

    A. Computers can be used to control temperature of plants.

    B. Computers can help you do such housework as heating up water.

    C. Internet can help you send and receive mails.

    D. Internet can design the flight course of space shuttle.

🔊 *Now watch the video twice and complete the sentences by filling in the blanks numbered 1 to 7 with the words and phrases you have just watched. At the end of this task, there will be a pause for you to check what you've written.*

It will be much more (1) _____ than spending a lot of time traveling to work every day. People will be able to use the video phone for (2) _____. They will be able to do (3) _____ and send them by mail or by fax. Computers will be used more and more in (4) _____. Railways in Japan already use them to work out to the best distance between trains. Trains will be (5) _____ by computer and many of them will have no drivers. Space travel will become much cheaper. In 1993, a new space rocket with no wings was developed in the USA. This type of rocket is able to return to the earth and land on its (6) _____. As a result, costs will be (7) _____ by as much as 90 percent.

VI   Listening Skills

1. The skills of dictating broadcasting news

(1) The significance of news dictation

(2) Introduction to famous foreign radios (VOA)

(3) Skills

   ① Prepare for English-Chinese and Chinese-English dictionaries.

   ② Play the listening material for the first time and get the whole picture of it.

   ③ Play the material sentence by sentence or word by word and try to have a dictation.

   ④ Play the word you don't know again and again, and try every other means to find the exact word.

   Means to catch the word:

   ★ Context clues;

   ★ Pronunciation rules.

   ⑤ Play the unfamiliar word for at least 50 times.

2. Sample practice

3. Additional training

I

Preview Exercises

1. Dictation:

Directions: *Listen and dictate what you've heard.*

_____

_____

_____

_____

2. Questions:

(1) What do the people think of Christmas nowadays?

_____

_____

_____

_____

(2) Who gave birth to Jesus?

_____

_____

_____

_____

II

Warming up Exercises

Background knowledge

1. A brief introduction to Christmas
   (1) The origin of Christmas.
   (2) The important characters related to Christmas.
2. Check the preview exercises
3. Other important festivals in the west

III   Listening Material

Directions: *In this part, you are going to listen to a passage. When you listen to it for the first time, you should pay attention to its main idea and answer some general comprehension questions. When you listen to it for the second time, you should focus on important details and answer some specific comprehension questions. When the passage is repeated for the third and the fourth time, you should complete the dictation task.*

Glossary

(1) pregnant   *adj.* 怀孕的

(2) fiancé   *n.* 未婚夫

(3) righteous   *adj.* 正直的,公义的

(4) engagement   *n.* 婚约

(5) disgrace   *v.* 使……失体面

(6) conceive   *v.* 怀孕

(7) prophet   *n.* 预言,先知

(8) decree   *v.* 发布命令

(9) census   *n.* 户口普查

(10) descendant   *n.* 后裔

(11) swaddle   *v.* 襁褓

(12) manger   *n.* 马槽

Task 1

Now listen to the passage for the first time and answer questions 1 to 2.

(1) What is the passage mainly about?

    A. About Jesus Christ and his father.

    B. About the origin of Christmas Day.

    C. About the birth of Jesus Christ.

    D. About Maria and Joseph's engagement.

(2) Where did Joseph go with Mary?

    A. Bethlehem in Judea.

    B. Nazareth in Galilee.

    C. Augustus in Rome.

    D. Anno Domini in Latin America.

Now listen to the passage for the second time and answer questions 3 to 5.

(3) What is the relationship between Mary and Joseph?

    A. Fiancé and fiancée.

    B. Husband and wife.

    C. Brother and sister.

    D. Mother and son.

(4) What did the angel ask Joseph to do?

    A. To marry Mary because she is a nice girl.

    B. To break the engagement with Mary because she is pregnant.

    C. To marry Mary for the baby within her has been conceived by Holy Spirit.

    D. To break the engagement with her because the baby is not his.

(5) Which of the following is NOT true?

    A. Joseph met an angel while thinking about the problem on his way home.

    B. Joseph had to go to Bethlehem to register for the census.

    C. Before the year 354, Jesus' birthday was celebrated on different dates.

    D. While Mary was a virgin, she was pregnant.

Task 3

Now listen to part of the passage twice and complete the dictation task by filling in the blanks numbered 1 to 10 with the exact words or sentences, or with the main points in your own words. At the end of this task, there will be a pause for you to check what you've written.

Now this is the story of how Jesus the "Messiah" was born. In Nazareth, a village in Galilee, his mother, Mary, (1) _____ to Joseph. But while she was still a (2) _____, she became (3) _____ by the Holy Spirit. Joseph, her fianc, being a (4) _____ man, decided to (5) _____ quietly, so as not to (6) _____ her publicly. As he considered this, he fell asleep, and an angel of the Lord appeared to him in a dream. "Joseph, son of David," the angel said, "Do not be afraid to (7)_____, for the child within her has been conceived by the Holy Spirit. And she will have a son, and you are to name him Jesus, (8) _____. All of this happened to (9) _____ through his prophet: Look! The virgin will conceive a child! She will (10) _____ a son. And he will be called Immanuel. "

When Joseph woke up, he did what the angel of the Lord commanded.

IV   Additional Listening Material

Directions: *In this part, you are going to listen to a passage. When you listen to it for the first time, you should pay attention to its main idea and answer some general comprehension questions. When you listen to it for the second time, you should focus on important details and answer some specific comprehension questions. When the passage is repeated for the third and the fourth time, you should complete the dictation task.*

Glossary

(1) Pilgrims	*n.* 清教徒		(3) preschool	*n.* 幼儿园
(2) feast	*n.* 宴会		(4) strengthen	*v.* 加强

Task 1

Now listen to the passage for the first time and answer questions 1 to 2.

(1) When is Thanksgiving Day in the United States?

    A. November the 4th.

    B. The fourth Thursday in November.

    C. November the 21st.

    D. One of Thursdays in November.

(2) How was the first Thanksgiving Day celebrated in 1621?

    A. People helped the poor by offering the food.

    B. People gave pocket money to their children.

    C. People held a big dinner to thank Indians for help.

    D. People invited their parents to enjoy their food.

Now listen to the passage for the second time and answer questions 3 to 5.

(3) What are school children learning about Thanksgiving Day nowadays?

    A. How to invite people.

    B. How to express thanks to people.

    C. How to help people.

    D. How to share with people in need.

(4) What is the meaning of "a sense of community"?

    A. The ability to cope with difficulties independently.

    B. The ability to care about and share with others.

    C. The ability to behave oneself responsibly.

    D. The ability to show great concern for family members.

(5) What is your understanding of Thanksgiving Day according to the passage?

    A. It is a day on which the rich deliver some money and food to the poor.

    B. It is a kind of practice to enforce the awareness of community.

    C. It is an excellent time to remind American people of their history.

    D. It is an occasion on which children learn to cook for their parents.

Task 3

Now listen to part of the passage twice and complete the dictation task by filling in the blanks numbered 1 to 10 with the exact words or sentences, or with the main points in your own words. At the end of this task, there will be a pause for you to check what you've written.

The fourth Thursday in November is Thanksgiving Day in the United States. Tradition says early English settlers known as the (1) _____ held the first celebration in 1621 in Plymouth, Massachusetts. They invited local Indians to a (2) _____ to thank them for help in (3) _____.

So what are schoolchildren learning these days about Thanksgiving?

Sharon Biros is a first-grade teacher in Clairton, Pennsylvania. Her students learn about the holiday as they discuss (4) _____. They read stories about the Indians and the Pilgrims. And the children tell (5)_____.

Many of the families are poor. The school (6) _____ a project in which students bring food and money to (7) _____.

Brook Levin heads a (8) _____ in Broomall, Pennsylvania. She says the kids learn about native culture Thanksgiving, she says, is a good time to (9) _____. The children make bread and other foods and invite their parents to school to enjoy them.

Thanksgiving is used as a time to (10) _____ a sense of community.

V Video-aural Material

Directions: *In this part, you are going to watch a video clip. When you watch the video for the first time, you should pay attention to its main idea and answer some general comprehension questions. When it is played for the second and the third time, you should complete the sentences with the words or phrases you have just watched.*

Glossary

(1) evoke *v.* 唤起	(13) bishop *n.* 主教
(2) underneath · *prep.* 在……下面	(14) canonize *v.* 尤指罗马天主教)把（死者）封为圣人
(3) bombard *v.* 炮击	(15) saint *n.* 圣徒
(4) nativity *n.* 诞生,出生	(16) revered *adj.* 推崇的
(5) nutcracker *n.* 胡桃钳	(17) generosity *n.* 慷慨
(6) explode *v.* 爆发,激发	(18) cathedral *n.* 大教堂
(7) kaleidoscope *n.* 万花筒	(19) remarkable *adj.* 显著的,异常的
(8) jolly *adj.* 开心的	(20) patron *n.* 守护人
(9) chubby *adj.* 胖嘟嘟的	(21) proximity *n.* 接近
(10) embellishment *n.* 装饰	(22) notion *,n.* 观念
(11) emerge *v.* 浮现,呈现	(23) phantom *n.* 幽灵
(12) evolution *n.* 发展	(24) dole *v.* 发放

👁 *Now watch the video for the first time and answer questions 1 to 2.*

(1) Why did Nicolas gradually become associated with Christmas?

    A. Because the date of Nicholas' death was honored every year.

    B. Because his notion of a phantom gift giver was widely accepted.

    C. Because he became a revered symbol of generosity.

    D. Because there were so many churches named after Nicholas.

(2) What became part of the tradition for Christmas in France in 12th Century?

    A. Giving children presents in their shoes.

    B. Giving children presents in their pockets.

    C. Exchanging presents to each other.

    D. Having a feast for Christmas.

Task 2

👁 *Now watch the video for the second time and answer questions 3 to 5.*

(3) What can impress you deeply in your memory for Christmas according to the clip?

    A. A grand Christmas dinner.

    B. A host of vivid images.

    C. Santa's funny appearance.

    D. Russian patron saints.

(4) What is Tim Cunningham according to the clip?

A. Actor.　　　B. Musician.　　　C. Postman.　　　D. Monk.

(5) Which of the following statements is NOT mentioned in the video?

A. Santa Claus is a fat and happy man.

B. On Christmas Day, people will put presents under the Christmas tree.

C. Christmas is a holiday only for children.

D. Nicholas was a bishop by the time he died around 350 AD.

Task 3

Now watch the video twice and complete the sentences by filling in the blanks numbered 1 to 7 with the words and phrases you have just watched. At the end of this task, there will be a pause for you to check what you've written.

(1) For most of us, the season evolves a kind of _____.

(2) My strongest memory of Christmas is _____.

(3) Christmas comes with a host of _____.

(4) Santa Claus is the _____.

(5) Santa's origins go back _____.

(6) The legend begins with the _____ Saint Nicholas.

(7) The real figure is famous for his _____ to _____.

VI　　Listening Skills

Listening Comprehensive Practice(1)

1. Short conversations

(1) A. See a doctor.

B. Stay in bed for a few days.

C. Get treatment in a better hospital.

D. Make a phone call to the doctor.

(2) A. At a publishing house.

B. At a bookstore.

C. In a reading room.

D. In Prof. Jordan's office.

(3) A. She used to be in poor health.

B. She was somewhat overweight.

C. She was popular among boys.

D. She didn't do well at high school.

(4) A. She sold all her furniture before she moved house.

B. She still keeps some old furniture in her new house.

C. She plans to put all her old furniture in the basement.

D. She bought a new set of furniture from Italy last month.

(5) A. Priority should be given to listening.

B. It's most helpful to read English newspapers every day.

C. It's more effective to combine listening with reading.

D. Reading should come before listening.

(6) A. The man enjoys traveling by car.

B. The man lives far from the subway.

C. The man is good at driving.

D. The man used to own a car.

(7) A. They will be replaced by on-line education sooner or later.

B. They will attract fewer kids as on-line education expands.

C. They will continue to exist along with on-line education.

D. They will limit their teaching to certain subjects only.

(8) A. They are both anxious to try Italian food.

B. They are likely to have dinner together.

C. The man will treat the woman to dinner tonight.

D. The woman refused to have dinner with the man.

(9) A. The exam was easier than the previous one.

    B. Joe is sure that he will do better in the next exam.

    C. Joe probably failed in the exam.

    D. The oral part of the exam was easier than the written part.

(10) A. She contacts her parents occasionally.

    B. She phones her parents regularly at weekends.

    C. She visits her parents at weekends when the fares are down.

    D. She often call her parents regardless of the rates.

2. Long conversations

Conversation 1

(1) A. To go boating on the St. Lawrence River.

    B. To go sightseeing in Quebec Province.

    C. To call on a friend in Quebec City.

    D. To attend a wedding in Montreal.

(2) A. Study the map of Quebec Province.

    B. Find more about Quebec Province.

    C. Brush up on her French.

    D. Learn more about the local customs.

(3) A. It's most beautiful in summer.

    B. It has many historical buildings.

    C. It was greatly expanded in the 18th century.

    D. It's the only French-speaking city in Canada.

Conversation 2

(1) A. An employee in the city council at Birmingham.

    B. Assistant Director of the Admissions Office.

    C. Head of the Overseas Students Office.

    D. Secretary of Birmingham Medical School.

(2) A. Nearly fifty percent are foreigners.

    B. About fifteen percent are from Africa.

C. A large majority are from Latin America.

D. A small number are from the Far East.

(3) A. She will have more contact with students.

    B. It will bring her capability into fuller play.

    C. She will be more involved in policy-making.

    D. It will be less demanding than her present job.

3. Compound dictation

Passage 1

There are a lot of good cameras available at the moment-most of these are made in Japan but there are also good (1) _____ models from Germany and the USA. We have (2) _____ a range of different models to see which is the best (3) _____ for money. After a number of different tests and interviews with people who are (4) _____ with the different cameras being assessed, our researchers (5) _____ the Olympic BY model as the best auto-focus camera available at the moment. It costs $200 although you may well want to spend more—(6) _____ as much as another $200—on buying (7) _____ lenses and other equipment. It is a good Japanese camera, easy to use. (8) _____, whereas the American versions are considerably more expensive. The Olympic BY model weighs only 320 grams which is quite a bit less than other cameras of a similar type. Indeed one of the other models we looked at weighed almost twice as much. (9) _____. All the people we interviewed expressed almost total satisfaction with it. (10) _____.

Passage 2

It's difficult to imagine the sea ever running out of fish. It's so vast, so deep, so (1) _____ ____. Unfortunately, it's not bottomless. Over-fishing, (2) _____ with destructive fishing practices, is killing off the fish and (3) _____ their environment.

Destroy the fish, and you destroy the fishermen's means of living. At least 60 (4) _____ of the world's commercially important fish (5) _____ are already over-fished, or fished to the limit. As a result, governments have had to close down some areas of sea to commercial fishing.

Big, high-tech fleets (6) _____ that everything in their path is pulled out of water. Anything too small, or the wrong thing, is thrown back either dead or dying. That's an (7) _____ of more than 20 million metric tons every year. (8) _____.

In some parts of the world, for every kilogram of prawns (对虾) caught, up to 15 kilograms of unsuspecting fish and other marine wildlife die, simply for being in the wrong place at the wrong time.

True, (9) _____ , but it's vital we find a rational way of fishing. Before every ocean becomes a dead sea, (10) _____ , then catch them in a way that doesn't kill other innocent sea life.

Passage 3

If you are a young college student, most of your concerns about your health and happiness in life are probably (1) _____ on the present. Basically, you want to feel good physically, mentally, and (2) _____ now. You probably don't spend much time worrying about the (3) _____ future, such as whether you will develop heart disease, or (4) _____, how you will take care of yourself in your (5) _____ years, or how long you are going to live. Such thoughts may have (6) _____ your mind once in a while. However, if you are in your thirties, forties, fifties, or older, such health-related thoughts are likely to become (7) _____ important to you.

(8) _____ , that will help you feel better physically and mentally. Recently researchers have found that, even in late adulthood, exercise, strength training with weights, and better food can help elderly individuals significantly improve their health and add happiness to their life. (9) _____ , giving us the opportunity to avoid some of the health problems that have troubled them. (10) _____.

I

Preview Exercises

1. Dictation:

Directions: *Listen to a passage and dictate what you've heard.*

_____

_____

_____

_____

2. Questions:

(1) What kind of transportation do you or your family usually take? Which one should be advocated?

_____

_____

_____

_____

(2) Try to list some advantages or disadvantages about private car and public transportation.

	Public Transportation	Private Transportation
Advantages		
Disadvantages		

II

Warming up Exercises

Background knowledge

1. A brief introduction to environmental protection

(1) Famous natural disasters in history and their courses.

(2) Development of modern environmental protection.

2. Check the preview exercises

Listening Material

Directions: *In this part, you are going to listen to a material. When you listen to the report for the first time, you should pay attention to its main ideas and answer some general comprehension questions. When you listen to it for the second time, you should focus on important details and answer some specific comprehension questions. When the report is repeated for the third and the fourth time, you should complete the dictation task.*

Task 1

🔊 *Now listen to the material for the first time and answer questions 1 to 2.*

(1) What is this passage mainly about?

    A. How to find better ways to protect our world in daily life.

    B. How to throw away the garbage.

    C. How to produce what we are using now.

    D. How to reduce global warming.

(2) Using the things wisely _____ .

    A. should be practiced by people of the developing country.

    B. will be beneficial only for present people.

    C. can help advanced societies develop rapidly.

    D. can do us a lot of good economically and ecologically.

Task 2

🔊 *Now listen to the material for the second time and answer questions 3 to 5.*

(3) Why do the speaker suggest we buy in large quantities?

    A. It is much cheaper.

    B. It can be stored for future use.

    C. It can reduce garbage.

    D. It is convenient for a big family.

(4) How to understand "One man's trash is another man's treasure."

    A. One man takes another man's fortune as a garbage.

B. What a person rejects might be very precious for another one.

C. Trash is not as important as treasure.

D. Treasure and trash are both important in people's mind.

(5) Which of the followings can be regarded as recycling?

A. Turn off the lights when you don't want to use them.

B. Give things that you don't want to other people.

C. Fix your old broken bicycle in your spare time.

D. Make the old clothes that you can't wear as a duster cloth.

Task 3

Now listen to the material twice and complete the dictation task by filling in the blanks numbered 1 to 10 with the exact words or sentences, or with the main points in your own words. At the end of this task, there will be a pause for you to check what you've written.

Did you know that there is a simple way we can reduce our waste by almost 50%? This is an important question to consider because the more waste that is burned, the more pollution we have. Reducing waste, therefore, is the key to reducing pollution. By following the simple (1)_____—"Reduce, Reuse, Recycle", we can make good use of what we have and (2)_____ the amount of waste and pollution.

First of all, we should reduce how much we use. We should only buy what we will use and use what we have bought. Also consider that buying products in larger (3)_____ can reduce garbage. For example, buying a large (4)_____ of toothpaste or a large bottle of dish soap instead of a small one helps reduce waste. Try also to reduce our energy use. Turning off lights in the house when we are not using them helps save (5)_____ energy.

Secondly, we should reuse what we have. Instead of throwing something away, we might give it away. There is an expression, "One man's trash is another man's (6)_____."
(7)_____ In addition, we can reuse plastic bags from the supermarket. Of course, instead of throwing away a broken item, we should fix it!

How and why: _____

_____

_____

3. Additional training

Directions: *In this section, you will hear a passage three times. When the passage is read for the first time, you should listen carefully and memorize its general idea in your mind. When the passage is read for the second time, you are required to write down the basic information you have just heard. Finally, when the passage is read for the third time, you should check what you have written.* 🔊

Who: _____

Identity: _____

When: _____

What programs: _____

_____

One of them is called _____

Details of this program:

Function: _____

Influence: _____

Major success: _____

Honor: _____

Preview Exercises

1. Dictation:

Directions: *Listen and dictate what you've heard.*

Catherine: _____

_____

_____

_____

Razia: _____

_____

_____

_____

2. Questions:

List some words and phrases to describe the opening ceremony.

_____

_____

_____

_____

_____

_____

Warming up Exercises

Background knowledge

1. A brief introduction to the Olympic Games

   (1) The introduction about the ancient Olympics and the modern Olympics.

   (2) The differences between the ancient Olympics and the modern Olympics.

2. Check the preview exercises

B. To visit a friend.

C. To attend a meeting.

D. To watch the grass roofs.

(5) According to Clinton, what happened in America?

A. Americans never pay attention to environmental protection.

B. Americans are far ahead of people in other countries in environmental protection.

C. Americans take pride in what they have done in environmental protection.

D. Americans are very interested in greening their house roofs.

Task 3

👀 *Now watch the video twice and complete the sentences by filling in the blanks numbered 1 to 5 with the words and phrases you have just watched. At the end of this task, there will be a pause for you to check what you've written.*

(1) A local historian says, because of the lack of _____ on the islands, the Vikings used grass on their roofs to provide stability and extra insulation.

(2) He says young people on the islands continue to build their houses with traditional grass roofs, not only to _____, but also because there are _____.

(3) To keep holding this made mechanical, and then you have to put this fishnet here, and this will be _____.

(4) He says, if a house has _____, the grass would produce e-nough _____ for one person per day.

(5) It's an old tradition in the Faroe Islands, so we asked our architect to get some solutions, where we could combine this _____, that (went) well together with this _____.

Listening Skills

1. The skills of note taking (1)

(1) What is note taking?

Note taking is the practice of writing down some pieces of information, often in an informal or unstructured manner.

(2) The significance of note-taking notes.

Mastering the skills of note-taking is very essential in listening. It can:

★ help you grasp the basic structure of the whole passage;

★ enable you to get the main idea;

★ give you some hints in completing every single information.

(3) Steps in mastering this skill.

① Recognize the main idea of the recording through the title;

② Try to catch the general idea of the passage or dialogue while listening for the first time, because understanding is more important for the next-step note-taking. Write down some important information rather than every single word;

③ Attach importance to the information following after the signal words or phrases like but, because, however, first, second, etc;

④ Select relevant information instead of everything while listening like what, when, where, who, why, how, etc;

⑤ Practice more and try to write down key information as fast as you can.

2. Sample practice

Directions: *In this section, you will hear a passage three times. When the passage is read for the first time, you should listen carefully and memorize its general idea in your mind. When the passage is read for the second time, you are required to write down the basic information you have just heard. Finally, when the passage is read for the third time, you should check what you have written.*

Who: _____

What: _____

When: _____

ago. The loss of trees upsets the (4) _____ as trees are necessary to build top-soil, maintain rainfall in dry climates, (5) _____ underground water and to (6) _____ carbon dioxide to oxygen. Trees bring water up from the ground, allowing water to (7) _____ into the atmosphere. The evaporated water then returns as rain, which is (8) _____ to areas that are naturally dry. Areas downwind of deforested lands lose this source of rainfall and are (9) _____ into deserts. Global warming results from the burning of fossil fuels, such as petroleum products, (10) _____

_____.

Carbon dioxide and other greenhouse gases then trap heat, resulting in warming of our atmosphere.

V   Video-aural Material

Directions: *In this part, you are going to watch a video clip. When you watch the clip for the first time, you should pay attention to its main ideas and answer some general comprehension questions. When you watch it for the second time, you should focus on important details and answer some specific comprehension questions. When the video is repeated for the third and the fourth time, you should complete the dictation task.*

Glossary

（1）aesthetic *adj.* 美学的	（4）insulation *n.* 隔离
（2）filter *v.* 过滤	（5）membrane *n.* 薄膜
（3）incorporate *v.* 包含,吸收	（6）Vikings *n.* 北欧海盗

Task 1

👁 *Now watch the video for the first time and answer questions 1 to 2.*

（1）According to the video, why did Vikings use grass on their roofs?

    A. Because they were very good at planting grass.

    B. Because there were not enough natural resources.

    C. Because they liked the color green very much.

    D. Because the grass roofs were very cheap.

（2）What is the main idea of this passage?

    A. People in Faeroe Island build green grass roofs.

    B. The history of Faeroe Island.

    C. The former US president Bill Clinton's trip to Faroe Island.

    D. The process of making grass roofs.

Task 2

👁 *Now watch the video for the second time and answer questions 3 to 5.*

（3）What do we know about grass roofs?

    A. 150 square meters of grass roofing would produce enough oxygen for one family per day.

    B. Grass roofs can filter pollutants and CO_2 out of the air.

    C. Young people in Faeroe Island still build houses with grass roofs because they think it is beautiful.

    D. We can make grass roofs simply by growing grass.

（4）Why did Bill Clinton go to Faeroe Island?

    A. To have a sight-seeing.

84

Finally, we can protect our world by recycling the products we have. Many materials can be used again to make something else. Soda bottles, paper products, plastic bags, (8)_____ ____, jars, and tires are just a few examples of (9)_____ items.

Protecting our world is the responsibility of every person. Reducing, reusing, and recycling are not only (10)_____ to us but will also be for the generations to come. Wisely using the things we have will not only help us save money but also help to save our earth.

IV	# Additional Listening Material

Directions: *In this part, you are going to listen to a report. When you listen to the report for the first time, you should pay attention to its main ideas and answer some general comprehension questions. When you listen to it for the second time, you should focus on important details and answer some specific comprehension questions. When the report is repeated for the third and the fourth time, you should complete the dictation task.*

Glossary

(1) carbon dioxide *n.* 二氧化碳	(3) fossil fuels *n.* 化石燃料
(2) deforest *adj.* 砍伐山林	(4) petroleum *n.* 石油

Task 1

Now listen to the report for the first time and answer questions 1 to 2.

(1) What are the two speakers talking about?

    A. The release of green house gases.

    B. Two present environmental issues.

    C. The development of energy supply.

    D. The process of era potation.

(2) What is the relationship between the two speakers?

    A. Interviewer and interviewee.

B. Colleagues.

C. Teacher and student.

D. Strangers.

Task 2

🔊 *Now listen to the report for the second time and answer questions 3 to 5.*

(3) According to the speaker, trees can _____.

    A. provide shade for people.

    B. beautify the habitat of the living things.

    C. enrich natural resource for human beings.

    D. maintain the balance of ecosystem.

(4) Which of the following is *True* according to the dialogue?

    A. Human beings have cut down most of the trees in the world now.

    B. Carbon dioxide plays an important part in global warming.

    C. Deforested area without rainfall will definitely turn into desert.

    D. Trees can clean all the underground water.

(5) What will half of the trees cut down by mankind result in?

    A. More acid rains.

    B. The lack of fertile land.

    C. Warming of our atmosphere.

    D. More petroleum products.

Task 3

🔊 *Now listen to the report twice and complete the dictation task by filling in the blanks numbered 1 to 10 with the exact words or sentences, or with the main points in your own words. At the end of this task, there will be a pause for you to check what you've written.*

(*Dr. McKinley of Awareness Magazine interviews a group of experts on environmental issues.*)

M: Hello, Dr. Semkiw. In your research, what environmental issues do you find most
    (1) _____?

W: Two environmental issues that we find most pressing are (2) _____ and
    (3) _____. Mankind has now cut down half of the trees that existed 10000 years

(5) What does the word "promotion" mean in the video?

    A. The promotion of the highest level of the sports performance.

    B. The promotion of the organization of the Olympic Games.

    C. The promotion of the Olympic Games towards the audience in the world.

    D. The promotion of the athletes who participate in the Olympic Games.

Task 3

👁 *Now watch the video twice and complete the sentences by filling in the blanks numbered 1 to 4 with the words and phrases you have just watched. At the end of this task, there will be a pause for you to check what you've written.*

(1) What is the first criterion?

    First of all, the Games should be held in _____.

(2) What does good organization include?

    And then, after that, you look at _____, which includes ____

    _____.

(3) What is concerned when all has been achieved?

    When all of that is been achieved, then you look at _____.

(4) Which criterion comes first?

    But among those criteria, _____ will come first. They are _____

    _____.

Ⅵ   Listening Skills

1. The skills of note taking (2)

(1) Note-taking in CET – 4, CET – 6, TEM – 8 and TEM – 8

Note-taking is the basic skill in listening. The answers to the questions are based on the information which the listeners get in note-taking. Note-taking skill is widely used in the English tests like CET – 4, CET – 6, TEM – 8 and TEM – 8. And the skill is introduced in various forms.

In CET – 4 and CET – 6, the listeners are required to fill in some missing information with the words and sentences they have heard. For the words, they should write down the exact words they have heard; for the sentences, they could either use the exact words or write down the main points with their own words.

In TEM – 4, the listeners are required to write down a passage with the exact words they have heard after listening for four times.

In TEM – 8, the listeners are required to complete gap fillings in a mini lecture after listening for only once. They could either use the exact words they have heard or fill in the gaps with their own words.

Although the forms of the tests are different, note taking skill is necessary in these tests.

(2) Skills for the note taking of the details
Attach importance to the information following after the signal words or phrases like but, because, however, first, second, etc.

Select relevant information instead of everything while listening like what, when, where, who, why, how, etc.

Have a good way of note taking that works well for you: use some note taking techniques. Such as: spacing between points, ordered points, keywords only, etc.

2. Sample practice

Directions: *In this section, you will hear a conversation three times. When the conversation is read for the first time, you should listen carefully for its general idea. When the conversation is read for the second time, you are required to fill in the blanks from 1 to 2 with the exact words you have just heard. For blanks numbered from 4 to 8 you are required to fill in the missing information. For these blanks, you can either use the exact words you have just heard or write down the main points in your own words. Finally, when the conversation is read for the third time, you should check what you have written.*

The Olympic flag measures (1)_____, (2)_____ and is completely white with five circles in the center. (3)_____

_____. (4)_____

_____. The white background symbolizes (5)_____. The five rings re-
present the five continents of the world:

(6)_____.

(7)_____.

(8)_____.

(9)_____.

(10)_____.

V | Video-aural Material

Directions: *In this part, you are going to watch a video clip. When you watch the video for the
first time, you should pay attention to its main ideas and answer some general
comprehension questions. When it is played for the second and the third time, you
should complete the sentences with the words or phrases you have just watched.*

Dr Jacques Rogge,
President of the IOC

Glossary

Task 1

👁 *Now watch the video for the first time and answer questions 1 to 2.*

(1) What is the video mainly about?

   A. Security is the most important factor which influence the Games

   B. IOC pays more attention to athletes' satisfaction and happiness.

   C. Mr. Rogge analyzes the factors that influence the success of the Games.

   D. The success of Beijing Olympic Games depends on many factors.

(2) What can you learn from the video?

   A. The Games which measures up to the factors must be a successful one.

   B. Only one factor could have great influence on the success of the Games.

   C. Beijing Olympic Games is very successful according to Mr. Rogge.

   D. The successful Games should measure up to many factors.

Task 2

👁 *Now watch the video for the second time and answer questions 3 to 5.*

(3) What is the most important criterion to the success of the Games according to Rogge?

   A. Highest level in sports performances.

   B. Security in peaceful environment for the Games.

   C. Athletes' satisfaction and happiness.

   D. Modern facilities in the Olympic Village.

(4) What do the personal issues refer to?

   A. Promotion and the number of the audience.

   B. Athletes' gold medals and new world records.

   C. Convenient transportation and good services.

   D. Security and the care of the athletes.

tion at the 1920 Games. But these words should not be understood simplistically as a call for unfettered (4)_____ of man's physical performances, but rather as (5)_____ _____. The Olympic Motto supposes the progress of human capacity on the basis of (6)_____ _____ improvement of man's natural qualities.

The sense of the Motto is that being first is not necessarily a (7)_____, but that giving one's best and (8)_____ is a worthwhile goal. It can not only apply to the individual athlete who makes great (9)_____ in his or her chosen field, but also apply to sports bodies, clubs, organizations and even states committed to the (10)_____ of modern Olympics.

IV Additional Listening Material

Directions: *In this part, you are going to listen to a passage. When you listen to the passage for the first time, you should pay attention to its main ideas and answer some general comprehension questions. When you listen to it for the second time, you should focus on important details and answer some specific comprehension questions. When the passage is repeated for the third and the fourth time, you should complete the dictation task.*

Glossary

(1) engrave *v.* 雕刻	(5) debut *n.* 第一次演出
(2) altar *n.* 祭坛	(6) incorporate *v.* 包含进去
(3) memorialize *v.* 纪念	(7) parade *n.* 游行
(4) emblem *n.* 象征	(8) alphabetical order 按字母顺序

Task 1

Now listen to the passage for the first time and answer questions 1 to 2.

(1) What is the passage mainly about?

　　A. The debut of the champions in Belgium.

B. The Olympic Rings and the Parade of the flags.

C. The Parade of flags and the original Olympic flag.

D. The Olympic Rings and the Olympic Flag.

(2) What can you learn from the passage?

A. The five-ring symbol engraved on an altar-stone was discovered by Coubertin.

B. The colors of the rings were chosen randomly.

C. The Olympic Flag was well known by the people around the world.

D. The original Olympic Flag is still used in the Olympic Games today.

Task 2

◁ *Now listen to the passage for the second time and answer questions 3 to 5.*

(3) Where did the five-ring symbol originate?

A. It came from an ancient building in Greece.

B. It came from an altar-stone at Delphi.

D. It came from a Greek legend.

D. It came from Antwerp, the 1920 Games.

(4) What are the 6 colors on the flag?

A. White, grey, red, green, blue and black.

B. White, golden, green, red, yellow and black.

C. White, purple, blue, yellow, red and black.

D. White, red, yellow, blue, green and black.

(5) Which flag is the first flag to enter the stadium in the Parade of flags?

A. The flag of the host country.

B. The Olympic Flag.

C. The flag of Greece.

D. The flag of the next host country.

Task 3

◁ *Now listen to the passage for the third time and complete the dictation task by filling in the blanks numbered 1 to 10 with the exact words or sentences either with exact words or its main i-deas in your own words. At the end of this task, there will be a pause for you to check what you've written.*

Listening Material

Directions: *In this part, you are going to listen to a passage. When you listen to the passage for the first time, you should pay attention to its main ideas and answer some general comprehension questions. When you listen to it for the second time, you should focus on important details and answer some specific comprehension questions. When the passage is repeated for the third and the fourth time, you should complete the dictation task.*

Glossary

(1) motto *n.* 格言	(11) commit *v.* 使承担义务
(2) embody *v.* 具体表达	(12) creed *n.* 信条
(3) abbot *n.* 修道士	(13) bishop *n.* 主教
(4) Dominican *adj.* 多米尼加的，[宗]多明我会的	(14) triumph *n.* 胜利
(5) priest *n.* 牧师	(15) spur *v.* 激励
(6) address to 对……说话	(16) embrace *v.* 信奉
(7) excel *v.* 胜过他人	(17) Didon 迪东
(8) inspire *v.* 激励	(18) Pierre de Coubertin 皮埃尔·顾拜旦
(9) unfettered *adj.* 不受拘束的	(19) Ethelbert Talbot 埃希贝尔特·塔尔博特
(10) essence *n.* 本质	

Task 1

Now listen to the passage for the first time and answer questions 1 to 2.

(1) What is the main idea of the passage?

A. It introduces the life history of the abbot Father Didon.

B. It introduces the place where all Olympic Games were held.

C. It introduces the Olympic Motto and Creed.

D. It introduces all the famous Olympic champions.

(2) What can you learn from the passage?

    A. The Olympic Motto and Creed were created by Coubertin.

    B. The meaning and values of the Olympic Spirit are conveyed by the Motto and Creed.

    C. The Olympic Motto is more popular than the Olympic Creed among people.

    D. The meaning of the Olympic Creed is much deeper than that of the Olympic Motto.

Task 2

🔊 *Now listen to the passage for the second time and answer questions 3 to 5.*

(3) Where does the creed come from?

    A. It comes from a sentence given by Coubertin.

    B. It comes from some words used by a Dominican priest.

    C. It comes from a speech given by Bishop Ethelbert Talbot.

    D. It comes from the International Olympic Charter.

(4) What did Coubertin use the phrase "Swifter, Higher, Stronger" for?

    A. Showing that the athletes can run faster, jump higher, and become stronger.

    B. Describing the great achievements at which the athletes should aim.

    C. Expressing the athlete's ambition to run faster, jump higher, and throw more strongly.

    D. Spurring the athletes to try their best to win more championships.

(5) What do the creed and motto mean?

    A. The athletes should win the championships in the Olympic Games.

    B. The athletes should defeat their opponents with their efforts.

    C. The athletes should surpass themselves in the Games.

    D. The athletes should believe in the Olympic Spirit and perform to their best.

Task 3

🔊 *Now listen to part of the passage twice and complete the dictation task by filling in the blanks numbered 1 to 10 with the exact words or sentences, or with the main points in your own words. At the end of this task, there will be a pause for you to check what you've written.*

According to the Olympic Charter, it (1)_____ the message which the IOC addresses to all who belong to the Olympic Movement, inviting them to excel (2)_____ the Olympic Spirit. This phrase has been inspiring modern (3)_____ since its introduc-

Glossary

(1) Terry Donovan　特里·多诺万	(8) Balaclava Street　巴拉克拉瓦街
(2) Jason Douglas　詹森·道格拉斯	(9) East. Ham　东罕(英国城市)
(3) Graham Smith　格雷厄姆·史密斯	(10) Hollywood　好莱坞
(4) Susan Fraser　苏珊·弗拉瑟	(11) brilliant　*adj.* 有才气的
(5) Stanley Hooper　史丹利·霍柏	(12) imitate　*v.* 模仿
(6) Maria Montrose　玛利亚·蒙特罗斯	(13) terrified　*adj.* 恐惧的
(7) Charles Orson　查尔斯·奥森	(14) furious　*adj.* 狂怒的

Complete the following resume for Jason Douglas.

Name：Jason Douglas

Former name：Graham Smith

Profession：(1) _____

Date of birth：(2) _____

1952：(3) _____

1958：(4) _____

1966：(5) _____

1969：(6) _____

1973：(7) _____

1974：(8) _____ with Maria Montrose

3. **Additional training**

Directions：*In this section, you will hear a passage three times. When the passage is read for the first time, you should listen carefully for its general idea. When the passage is read for the second time, you are required to fill in the blanks from1 to 15. For these blanks, you can either use the exact words you have just heard or write down the main points in your own words. Finally, when the passage is read for the third time, you should check what you have written.*

Glossary

(1) strain　*n.* 紧张	(10) infrequent　*adj.* 很少发生的
(2) previous　*adj.* 早前的	(11) incidental　*adj.* 偶然的
(3) infer　*v.* 推断	(12) abbreviate　*v.* 缩写
(4) solely　*adv.* 独自地	(13) maximum　*adj.* 最大限度的
(5) beforehand　*adv.* 预先	(14) neglect　*v.* 忽视
(6) explicitly　*adv.* 明确地	(15) lengthy　*adj.* 冗长的
(7) colloquial　*adj.* 通俗的	(16) conventional　*adj.* 常规的
(8) crunch　*n.* 紧要关头	(17) framework　*n.* 框架
(9) intonation　*n.* 语调	

Complete the following outline.

Title：Lectures and Note-taking

Skills of note taking：

Ⅰ. Understand what the lecturer says as he says it.

　A. It's difficult to understand a lecture.

　　1. Cannot stop (1) ＿＿＿＿＿＿＿＿＿＿＿.

　　2. May not recognize words which he understands in print.

　B. Solutions：

　　1. Infer (2) ＿＿＿＿＿＿＿＿＿＿.

　　2. Don't be discouraged if there is a failure in inferring.

　　3. Often possible to understand much by (3) ＿＿＿＿＿＿＿＿＿＿＿.

Ⅱ. What's important?

　A. Most important information is the title itself.

　　1. Make sure to write it down (4) ＿＿＿＿＿＿＿＿＿＿.

　　2. Implies (5) ＿＿＿＿＿＿＿＿＿＿＿.

　B. Direct signals & indirect signals.

　　1. direct signals：

　　　a. Explicit：the point is important and that the student should write it down.

　　　b. Colloquial：(6) ＿＿＿＿＿＿＿＿＿＿＿＿＿＿＿＿＿＿＿＿＿

　　　＿＿＿＿＿＿＿＿＿＿＿＿＿＿＿＿＿＿＿＿＿＿＿＿＿＿＿＿＿.

　　2. indirect signals：

a. Something important: pause, speak slowly, speak loudly, use a greater range of intonation, or employ a combination of these devices.

b. Something incidental: (7) _____.

III. Writing down the main points.

A. Use (8) _____.

B. Select only words which give maximum information, usually nouns and sometimes (9) _____.

C. Write (10) _____.

D. Time to write

　　1. Connectives that indicate the argument is proceeding in the same direction: write e. g. (11) _____.

　　2. Connectives that indicate (12) _____

_____: listen e. g. "however", "on the other hand" or "nevertheless".

IV. Show the connections between the various points by visual presentation.

A. spacing

B. (13) _____

C. (14) _____

D. (15) _____

I

Preview Exercises

1. Dictation (1):

Directions: *Listen and dictate what you've heard.*

_____

_____

_____

_____

2. Question (1):

In how many different ways can we pay our tuition? How do you pay your tuition?

_____

_____

_____

_____

3. Dictation (2):

Directions: *Listen and dictate what you've heard.*

_____

_____

_____

_____

4. Question (2):

What are the disadvantages and advantages of taking a part-time job as a university student?

_____

_____

_____

_____

II   Warming up Exercises

Background knowledge

1. Introduction to ways of paying tuitions fees, including taking part-time jobs
2. Your preferable way of paying tuition
3. Advantages and disadvantages of taking a part-time job as student
4. Check the preview exercises

III   Listening Material

Directions: *In this part, you are going to listen to a conversation. When listening for the first time, you should pay attention to its main idea and answer some general comprehension questions. When listening for the second time, please focus on important details and answer some specific comprehension questions. When part of the conversation is repeated for the third time, you should complete the dictation task.*

Glossary

(1) hectic adj. 兴奋的	(4) travel agency 旅行社
(2) sort of 有点	(5) freshman n. 大一学生
(3) tour guide 导游	(6) end up in doing sth. 最后最终

Task 1

 Now listen to the conversation for the first time and answer questions 1 to 2.

(1) What does Michael plan to do after graduation?

    A. He will take several part-time jobs first.

    B. He will go back to China and find a job there.

    C. He will work in the computer and network industry.

    D. He may look for a job in tourism sector.

(2) Why did the girl change her major?

    A. She couldn't get a scholarship if she pursued her previous major.

    B. Her parents were against her original choice.

    C. Her first major would make it rather difficult to get employed.

    D. She gradually lost interest in her previous major.

Task 2

◁ *Now listen to the conversation for the second time and answer questions 3 to 5.*

(3) How does the girl support herself financially on campus?

    A. She does a part time job in a travel agency.

    B. She has gained a four-year scholarship.

    C. She has been supported by her parents.

    D. She has applied for a bank loan to cover the tuition.

(4) When does Michel do his part time job?

    A. Every night.

    B. In the middle of the day.

    C. On weekends.

    D. During the summer vacation.

(5) How did Michel get the job at the travel agency?

    A. Most of the tourists are Chinese.

    B. The travel agency is in short of staffs.

    C. He did the job without being paid.

    D. He was familiar with the head of the agency.

Task 3

◁ *Now listen to the conversation twice and complete the dictation task by filling in the blanks numbered 1 to 10 with the exact words or sentences either with exact words or its main ideas in your own words. At the end of this task, there will be a pause for you to check what you've written.*

Boy: Hi, I saw you yesterday with John. We (1) _____ together, I'm Michael.

Girl: Oh ... hi, Mike! How are you doing?

Boy: I'm ok. But school's been really hectic since I came. I haven't even had a chance to (2) _____.

Girl: I know. It's especially (3) _____ when you are freshman. Hey, what's your major?

Boy: Traveling tourism.

Girl: Wow, what do you plan to do after you (4) _____?

Boy: Um ... I haven't really decided it. I think I like to work for a travel agency in this area. What about you?

Girl: Well, when I first (5) _____ college, I majored in physics. But later I realized that I'd have a hard time in finding a job in that field. I ended up in (6) _____ to computer science. Finding a job in the IT industry shouldn't be as difficult.

Boy: Have you got a part-time job to support yourself (7) _____ school?

Girl: Well, (8) _____.

Boy: Wow, lucky you!

Girl: Yeah. How about you! Are you paying for school yourself?

Boy: Sort of (9) _____.

Girl: A travel agency. (10) _____ What do you do there?

Boy: I'm a tour guide. I show tour groups around the city.

Girl: Wow! Your English must be pretty good then.

Boy: Actually. They are all Chinese tourists. That's why I got the job.

| IV | **Additional Listening Material** |

Directions: *In this part, you are going to listen to a conversation. When listening for the first time, you should pay attention to its main ideas and answer some general comprehension questions. When listening for the second time, please focus on important details and answer some specific comprehension questions. When part of the conversation is repeated for the third time, you should complete the dictation task.*

Glossary

(1) brochure *n.* 小册子	(4) compensation package 工资福利
(2) prospective *adj.* 潜在的	(5) candidate *n.* 应聘者
(3) dental coverage 牙齿护理保险	(6) entry-level 初级

Task 1

Now listen to the conversation for the first time and answer questions 1 to 2.

(1) Why does the interviewee's future job require much travel?

    A. This company is a travel agency.

    B. The man has to deliver goods of the company to customers.

    C. The company has many branches and subsidiaries.

    D. The man has to negotiate with potential customers.

(2) What's company's future sales plan?

    A. Online sales.

    B. Door-to-door sales.

    C. Expansion of international markets.

    D. Sales promotion to neighboring countries.

Task 2

Now listen to the conversation for the second time and answer questions 3 to 5.

(3) What can you infer from this conversation?

    A. The man failed in this job interview.

    B. The man gives up the job opportunity because of dissatisfaction.

    C. The woman is satisfied with the male candidate's performance.

    D. The interview result is not clear yet.

(4) What are the major parts of the compensation package?

    A. An annual salary of 30000 dollars.

    B. Physical health and dental coverage.

    C. Two weeks of paid vocation.

    D. All of the above.

(5) What will the man probably do after this interview?

    A. He may start to work on his new position.

    B. He may travel abroad to visit customers.

    C. He may be interviewed by the Sales Manager.

    D. He may have to look for jobs elsewhere.

Task 3

Now listen to the conversation twice and complete the dictation task by filling in the blanks numbered 1 to 10 with the exact words or sentences either with exact words or its main ideas in your own words. At the end of this task, there will be a pause for you to check what you've written.

Woman: I've asked you a lot of questions. Now do you have any questions about life (1) _____ or the position?

Man: Yes. Can you tell me about the company's future plans?

Woman: Yes. Our big (2) _____ now is on the internet sales. It's all printed in our company brochure. Here.

Man: Thank you, and who will be my (3) _____?

Woman: As a sale representative, you'll be working in a sales department. You report to the (4) _____ sales manager.

Man: And does the job require much travel?

Woman: Yes. Our sales people are on the road a lot, visiting (5) _____ customers. Any more questions?

Man: Um..., no, I can't think of things of any others at this time.

Woman: Well, let me give you some information about our (6) _____ package. We offer our entry-level sales people an (7) _____ salary of 30000 dollars, physical health and dental coverage and, (8) _____.

Man: That sounds good.

Woman: Well, Sean, I so enjoy meeting you. You seem a strong candidate for this position. (9) _____.

Man: Thank you very much.

Woman: Good luck and (10) _____.

V Video-aural Material

Directions: *In this part, you are going to watch a video clip. When you watch the video for the first time, you should pay attention to its main ideas and answer some general comprehension questions. When it is played for the second and the third and fourth time, you should complete the sentences with the words or phrases you have just watched.*

Glossary

(1) leadership　*n.* 领导能力　　　　(2) creatively　*adv.* 有创造性地

Task 1

👁 *Now watch the video for the first time and answer questions 1 to 2.*

(1) What are the woman and man talking about?

A. The necessity of a writing test.

B. Creativity skills in the company.

C. How to write a successful resume.

D. Screening the candidates.

(2) How does the first candidate impress the two interviewers?

A. He is not charming enough.

B. He lacks in a creativity skill the company needs.

C. He is in short of all the leadership skills.

D. He is very impressive in the interview.

Task 2

👁 *Now watch the video for the second time and answer questions 3 to 5.*

(3) How does the man think of the second candidate?

    A. Better than the third candidate.

    B. Better than the first candidate.

    C. Best of the three.

    D. Not very impressive.

(4) How does the woman think of the second candidate?

    A. She is very charming to the two interviewers.

    B. She is good at communicating with others.

    C. She is the best of all the candidates.

    D. She seems to be a hard-working person.

(5) Which candidate is singled out at last?

    A. The candidate who seems very charming.

    B. The candidate who is very serious to her work.

    C. The candidate who is a hard-working man.

    D. The candidate who is the winner in the written test.

Task 3

👁 *Now watch the video twice and complete the sentences by filling in the blanks numbered 1 to 5 with the words and phrases you have just watched. At the end of this task, there will be a pause for you to check what you've written.*

(1) I think he has more charm _____.

(2) She answered the questions we gave her _____.

(3) Yes, but that may mean she doesn't have the _____we are looking for.

(4) I cannot _____ him from the second one.

(5) It's a hard choice, and perhaps we should _____.

VI Listening Skills

1. The skill of shorthand (1)

We've learned a variety of listening skills from the previous units, such as note-taking, dictation, news listening, main idea, details, signal words and so on. In this unit, we'll focus on shorthand.

1. What is shorthand?

   Shorthand is a method of writing rapidly by using abbreviated or symbolic forms.
2. Shorthand in the dictation of TEM – 4.

   Shorthand is very important in the dictation of TEM – 4; it is convenient to take notes by abbreviated or symbolic forms of words in the limited time.
3. Skills:

   (1) Get hold of the general meaning of the whole passage for the first time.

   (2) The crucial factor is to grasp the symbols while listening for the second and third time; here come several types of symbols to help you:

Types	The meanings of symbols
English letters:	A: agriculture. agriculture B: business C×: conflict, confrontation C: government, govern P: politics, political E: total, totally, entire, entirely, on the whole, all in all K: fishery O: international, worldwide, global, universal, etc. J: pleasant, joyful, happy, excited, etc. L: unsatisfied, discomfort, angry, sad, etc. W: work, employ

Types	The meanings of symbols
Math symbols	+ : many, lots of, a great deal of, a good many of, etc. + + (+2) : more +3 : most − : little, few, lack , in short of/ be in shortage of, etc. × : wrong/incorrect, something bad, notorious, negative, etc. > : bigger/larger/greater/more than/better than, etc. < : less/smaller, etc. = : means, that is to say, in other words, the same as, be equal ( ) : among, within, etc. ≠ : be different from, etc. ~ : about/around, or so, approximately, etc. / : cross out, eliminate, etc.
Punctuation	? : question, issue "2m" : two month ago "y" : this year, "y2" : two year later, next week √ : right/good, famous/well-known, etc. ☆ : important, exemplary best, outstanding, brilliant, etc. & : and, together with, along with, accompany, along with, further more, etc. ‖ : end, stop, halt, bring sth to a standstill/stop, etc.
Abbreviation	-ism : socialism Sm -tion : standardization STDN -cian : technician techo -ing : marketing (MKTg) -ed : accepted acptd -able/ible/ble : available avbl -ment : amendment amdmt -ize : recognize regz -ful : meaningful mnfl

2. Sample practice

Directions: *In this section, you will hear a passage four times. When the passage is read for the first time, you should listen carefully for its general idea. When the passage is read for the second time and third time, you are required to dictate what you have just heard by symbols. Finally, when the passage is read for the fourth time, you should check what you have written.* ◁

_____

_____

_____

3. Additional training

Directions: *In this section, you will hear a passage four times. When the passage is read for the first time, you should listen carefully for its general idea. When the passage is read for the second time and third time, you are required to dictate what you have just heard by symbols. Finally, when the passage is read for the fourth time, you should check what you have written.* ◁

Glossary

(1) abnormality *n.* 反常,异常	(3) tier *n.* 列,行
(2) gorge *n.* 峡谷	(4) affect *n.* 影响,作用

_____

_____

_____

_____

I

Preview Exercises

1. Dictation:

Directions: *Listen and dictate what you've heard.*

_____
_____
_____
_____
_____

2. Questions:

(1) List some words of earthquake.

_____
_____
_____
_____
_____

(2) List some sentences to describe earthquake.

_____
_____
_____
_____
_____

II

Warming up Exercises

Background knowledge

1. A brief introduction to earthquake

    (1) Expressions of Wenchuan earthquake.

    (2) Words of earthquake.

2. Check the preview exercises

Listening Material

Directions: *In this part, you are going to listen to a piece of news. When you listen to it for the first time, you should pay attention to its main ideas and answer two general comprehension questions. When you listen to it for the second time, you should focus on important details and answer some specific comprehension questions. When it is repeated for the third and the fourth time, you should complete the dictation task.*

Glossary

(1) residential *adj.* 住宅的

(2) dispatch *v.* 派遣

(3) victim *n.* 受害者

(4) autonomous *adj.* 自治的

(5) underneath *prep.* 在……下面

(6) rescue *v.* 援救,救出,营救

(7) viaduct *n.* 高架桥

(8) prefecture *n.* 县

Task 1

Now listen to the news for the first time and answer the question 1 to 2.

(1) When did the earthquake happen and who directed the rescue work?

 A. 2:28 p.m. on Monday, Premier Wen Jiabao.

 B. 2:28 a.m. on Wednesday, Premier Wen Jiabao.

 C. 2:28 p.m. on Monday, President Hu Jin Tao.

 D. 2:28 a.m. on Wednesday, President Hu Jin Tao.

(2) Where did the earthquake happen and how much magnitude of the earthquake?

 A. Mianzhou in Sichuan province, 7.8 on the Richter scale.

 B. Mianzhou in Sichuan province, 7.9 on the Richter scale.

 C. Wenchuan county in Sichuan province, 7.9 on the Richter scale.

 D. Wenchuan county in Sichuan province, 7.8 on the Richter scale.

Task 2

Now listen to the news for the second time and answer questions 3 to 5.

(3) What happened to telecommunication in Chendu after the quake?

 A. A little destroyed.

B. Safe.

C. Little damaged.

D. Down.

(4) How many provinces or cities are affected by this earthquake?

    A. 7.

    B. 8.

    C. 9.

    D. 6.

(5) Which of the facts on earthquake is true?

    A. A major earthquake measuring 7.8 on the Richter scale has hit Wenchuan county.

    B. Premier Wen Jiabao has ordered all – out efforts to rescue quake – hit victims.

    C. The incident took place at 2:28 p.m. on Wednesday.

    D. Many buildings collapsed in downtown Chengdu.

Task 3

Now listen to the news twice and complete the dictation task by filling in the blanks numbered 1 to 10 with the exact words or sentences, or with the main points in your own words. At the end of this task, there will be a pause for you to check what you've written.

A major earthquake measuring (1) _____ on the Richter scale has hit Wenchuan county in southwest China's Sichuan province.

President Hu Jintao has ordered all – out (2) _____ to rescue quake – hit victims. Premier Wen Jiabao was on his way to the hit area to direct the rescue work. Chengdu Military Area Command has dispatched troops to help with (3) _____ relief work in the earthquake – stricken county.

The incident happened at 2:28 p.m. on Monday. The (4) _____ of Wenchuan county lies in the Tibetan – Qiang Autonomous Prefecture of Aba, about 100 kilometers northwest of the provincial capital Chengdu. (5) _____ were also reported in many other parts of China, including Ningxia, Qinghai, Gansu, Chongqing, Hunan, Hubei, Shanxi, Shaanxi and Shanghai, and as far away as (6) _____ and Vietnam. Cracks were seen on walls of some

residential structures in downtown Chengdu, but no buildings (7) _____.
(8) _____. An underground water pipe was bro-
ken a viaduct close to Chengdu's southern railway station, and a road was flooded.
(9) _____. (10) _____.

<h1>IV   Additional Listening Material</h1>

Directions: *In this part, you are going to listen to a news. When you listen to the report for the first time, you should pay attention to its main ideas and answer some general comprehension questions. When you listen to it for the second time, you should focus on important details and answer some specific comprehension questions. When it is repeated for the third and the fourth time, you should complete the dictation task.*

Glossary

(1) survivors *n.* 幸存者   (3) equivalent *n.* 相等物
(2) Belgium *n.* 比利时[欧洲]   (4) fundraising *adj.* 筹措资金的

Task 1

 Now listen to the news for the first time and answer the questions 1 to 2.

(1) Who are showing their concern by pledging donations according to the news?

     A. Overseas Chinese in Belgium, Netherlands and Britain.

     B. All foreign friends from European countries.

     C. All Chinese students who are studying medicine.

     D. Many international fundraising organization.

(2) How much money did Chinese businesses in the Netherlands raise the equivalent in an hour?

     A. Exactly 360000 yuan.

     B. More than 360000 yuan.

     C. About 360000 yuan.

     D. Less than 360000 yuan.

Task 2

Now listen to the news for the second time and answer the questions 3 to 5.

(3) Who has called for all overseas Chinese to donate money to the earthquake survivors?

    A. Overseas Chinese.

    B. The Chinese Scholars.

    C. The Chinese Association.

    D. The Chinese Students Scholars Association in Britain.

(4) In which country did Chinese students donate?

    A. France.

    B. America.

    C. Belgium.

    D. Canada.

(5) Where did people from all walks of life donate their money?

    A. The University of Paris.

    B. The University of Oxford.

    C. The University of Cambridge.

    D. The University of London.

Task 3

Now listen to the news twice and complete the dictation task by filling in the blanks numbered 1 to 8 with the exact words. At the end of this task, there will be a pause for you to check what you've written.

Survivors equivalent Belgium (1) _____ Overseas Chinese, including businesses and students, are showing their concern by pledging donations.

Chinese businesses in the (2) _____ raised the equivalent of over 360000 yuan in an hour. They will hold more fundraising performances to (3) _____ Sichuan province.

In Belgium, over the past two days, Chinese students have (4) _____ in many ways, saying they will help in any way they can.

Chinese student in Brussels Ren Tao said, "I'm (5)_____ medicine and if my country needs my help, I would love to come back now. I'd like to do my best to (6)_____ and treat patients. "

The Chinese Students Scholars Association in Britain has called for all overseas Chinese to donate money to the earthquake (7)_____. At the University of London, not only the Chinese, but people from all walks of life have opened their (8)_____.

V Video-aural Material

Directions: *In this part, you are going to watch a video clip. When you watch the video for the first time, you should pay attention to its main ideas and answer some general comprehension questions. When it is played for the second time, you should answer the specific questions.*

Glossary

(1) impending *adj.* 逼迫的,迫切的	(4) enclosure *n.* 围墙,围绕
(2) surreal *adj.* 怪异的,可怕的	(5) horrendous *adj.* 可怕的,令人惊惧的
(3) tsunami *n.* 海啸	(6) geographic *adj.* 地理学上的(地区的)

👁 *Now watch the video for the first time and answer the question 1 to 2.*

(1) What kind of animal species can sense impending danger when the tsunami hit in 2004?

    A. Panda.

    B. Snake.

    C. Elephant.

    D. Mouse.

(2) What did the British tourist say while watching the pandas as the quake struck?

    A. They had been really lazy and just eaten a little bit of bamboo.

    B. Pandas were not prepared for parading around their pair.

    C. They looked back and were sure of abnormal things to happen.

    D. Pandas felt scared and ran to different directions.

Task 2

👁 *Now watch the video for the second time and answer the question 3 to 5.*

(3) Did the pandas in China's Wolong Reserve know that Monday's earthquake was coming before it hit?

    A. Yes.

    B. No.

    C. Not sure.

    D. No one knows.

(4) How many pandas were reported safe on Tuesday in Wolong?

    A. 85.

    B. 95.

    C. 96.

    D. 86.

(5) What happened according to this passage?

    A. Some scientists say animals can't sense impending danger.

    B. Some animal species have a greater awareness than humans of vibrations in the ground.

    C. A group of tourists was taken to the provincial capital of Chengdu on Friday morning.

D. Elephants can hear high frequency sound waves.

Task 3

👁️ *Now watch the video twice and complete the sentences by filling in the blanks numbered 1 to 7 with the words and phrases you have just watched. At the end of this task, there will be a pause for you to check what you've written.*

(1) A British tourist watching the pandas as the quake struck offered _____.

(2) Some scientists say animals can sense impending danger by detecting _____ in the environment.

(3) When the tsunami hit in 2004, there were reports that elephants in Sri Lanka fled to higher ground well before the waves _____.

(4) Some animal species have a greater awareness than humans of vibrations in the ground. And they may sense smaller tremors _____ a bigger earthquake.

(5) Twelve Americans, part of a World Wildlife _____ tour of China, were visiting the Panda Reserve in Wolong when the earthquake struck.

(6) The 7.9 magnitude earthquake hit on Monday with the _____ near Wolong Reserve.

(7) So far _____ stands at almost 20000 and is expected to climb higher as rescue efforts progress.

VI   Listening Skills

1. The skills of shorthand (2)

The purpose of listening and dictating exercises is to train students to listen and retrieve information, namely meaning from the source text. Students, however, tend to focus on words, phrases, expressions and other language forms while listening to the source text. Consequently, their comprehension of the source text becomes blurred when those linguistic symbols disappear. And that's why students find it rather difficult to balance listening and dictating at the same time.

Students can alleviate their memory burden when listening to the source text with the help of special notes, such as abbreviations, Chinese characters, symbols, etc. The following are the ways of some useful notes.

(1) Abbreviations

　　w: we

　　u: you

　　I: I

　　g: government

　　e: economy, economic

　　s: social, society

　　clg: challenge

　　p: policy, politics

　　nw: new

(2) Symbols

　　= equate, equal

　　> more than

　　÷ besides, except

　　∵ because, since

　　∴ so, consequently

　　↗ improve, increase

　　⊙ meeting, conference

　　# only, just

　　★ important, significant

　　∟ future

　　∞ relations

　　[ ] through, by means of

　　e. g. This meeting is very important to our future work.

　　　　　⊙

　　　　　　　　★

　　　　　　∟

We will further our bilateral relations through this new policy.

w

↗ 2 ∞

[nw p]

2. **Sample practice**

Now, listen and dictate the following passage according to the listening skills we've introduced in this unit.

_____

_____

_____

_____

_____

_____

_____

_____

_____

_____

3. **Additional training**

Now, listen and dictate the following news according to the listening skills we've introduced in this unit.

_____

_____

_____

_____

_____

_____

_____

_____

_____

Unit Twelve Shenzhou VII

Preview Exercises

1. Dictation:

Directions: *Listen and dictate what you've heard.*

_____

_____

_____

_____

_____

2. Questions:

(1) Why did teacher organize the students to watch the launch of China's Shenzhou VII space mission?

_____

_____

_____

_____

(2) Did you enjoy watching the launch of China's Shenzhou VII space mission? And why?

_____

_____

_____

_____

Warming up Exercises

Background knowledge

1. A brief introduction to space mission in China
2. Check the preview exercises

III   Listening Material

Directions: *In this part, you are going to listen to a live interpretation of the launch of Shenz-hou Ⅶ. When you listen to this program for the first time, you should pay attention to its main ideas and answer some general comprehension questions. When you listen for the second time, you should focus on important details and answer some specific comprehension questions. When the program is repeated for the third and fourth time, you should complete the dictation task.*

Glossary

(1) applaud *v.* 鼓掌

(2) real-time image 实况画面

(3) simulated image 模拟画面

(4) hereby *adv.* 因此，据此

(5) initial *adj.* 开始的，最初的

(6) implement *v.* 实现，执行

Task 1

Now listen to the program for the first time and answer questions 1 to 2.

(1) What do you know about Shenzhou Ⅶ?

    A. The launch of Shenzhou Ⅶ is the world's third launching activity.

    B. The launch of Shenzhou Ⅶ is the third manned space flight launching activity.

    C. Shenzhou Ⅶ is the first activity of spacewalk in the world.

    D. Shenzhou Ⅶ is the third activity of spacewalk in China.

(2) What phases does Shenzhou Ⅶ activity have?

    A. Waiting for launching, launching, spacewalk, and landing.

    B. Waiting for launching, launching, spacewalk, landing, and medical checking.

    C. Launching, spacewalk, landing, and medical checking.

    D. Launching, spacewalk, and landing.

Task 2

Now listen to the program for the second time and answer questions 3 to 5.

(3) What can you learn from the second time listening?

    A. Scientists have been working very hard for the past five years for the successful launching.

  B. President Hu Jingtao has been watching the process through TV relay.

  C. We can see the simulated image and the real one at the same time.

  D. Shenzhou Ⅶ is scheduled to enter its orbit to move around the earth one week.

(4) Where was Shenzhou Ⅶ launched?

  A. In Qingdao.

  B. In eastern China.

  C. In northwestern China.

  D. In Xichang, western China.

(5) What does "exciting moment" mean?

  A. The moment China launches the space shuttle.

  B. The moment China sends three astronauts into space.

  C. The moment to perform spacewalk by three Chinese astronauts.

  D. The moment to perform the first spacewalk in China.

Task 3

🔊 *Now listen to part of the program twice and complete the dictation task by filling in the blanks numbered 1 to 10 with the exact words or sentences either with exact words or its main ideas in your own words. At the end of this task, there will be a pause for you to check what you've written.*

"Comrade, Shenzhou Ⅶ spacecraft has successfully been launched. This (1) _____ the man space flight mission has achieved its initial success. On (2)_____ of the CPC Central Committee, the State Council , the Central Military (3) _____, I wish to send my deepest (4) _____ and respect to all those who have participated in this mission and congratulations. Implementing this man space flight mission is a (5) _____ mission for our country at state level in this year, in the science and technology field. It is another milestone in Chinese people's march towards as the science, and mission in space. This time Chinese astronauts, will participate in a spacewalk for the first time ever. And this means that the (6) _____ and technological difficulties have been raised to (7) _____ level. This has put greater pressure and request on the organization and total (8) _____ of this mission. After this (9) _____ has actually entered into orbit, (10)_____
_____ . "

Directions: *In this part, you are going to listen to a live interpretation of the launch of Shenzhou Ⅶ. When you listen to this program for the first time, you should pay attention to its main ideas and answer some general comprehension questions. When you listen for the second time, you should focus on important details and answer some specific comprehension questions. When the program is repeated for the third and fourth time, you should complete the dictation task.*

Glossary

(1) hatch *n.* 舱口	(6) backpack *n.* 背包
(2) EVA 空中行走	(7) bulgy *adj.* 臃肿的
(3) module *n.* 太空舱	(8) taikonaut *n.* 中国航天员
(4) capsule *n.* 飞船，太空舱	(9) vacuum *n.* 真空
(5) helmet *n.* 头盔	

Task 1

Now listen to the program for the first time and answer questions 1 to 2.

(1) What does this interpreter tell us?

　　A. He tells us how astronauts work in the space.

　　B. He introduces how the module works in the space.

　　C. He interprets the whole story about the spacewalk.

　　D. He describes the difficulties when the astronaut does the EVA.

(2) What can we learn from this interpretation?

　　A. It is very easy for the astronaut to go out of the module.

　　B. It is very difficult for the astronaut to go out of the module.

　　C. Going outside and inside the module must be carefully done.

　　D. Going back to the module is easier than going out of the module.

Task 2

Now listen to the program for the second time and answer questions 3 to 5.

(3) What·happened immediately when the hatch was opened?

  A. We can see the helmet.

  B. We can see the flag of PRC.

  C. We can see something flying out from the module.

  D. We can see the background of the earth.

(4) What did the astronaut do when he was ready to go back into the module?

  A. He collected tie lace and hooks.

  B. He loosened his backpack.

  C. He made the door widely opened.

  D. He asked his partner for help.

(5) What was the process of entering the module?

  A. His head should be first inside the module.

  B. His feet should be first into the module.

  C. It is the same with getting out of the module.

  D. It is opposite to getting out of the module.

Task 3

Now listen to part of the program twice and complete the dictation task by filling in the blanks numbered 1 to 7 with the exact words or sentences either with exact words or its main ideas in your own words. At the end of this task, there will be a pause for you to check what you've written.

He said, "I have been out of the hatch. I am feeling good. To all the people in my country, in the world, my (1) _____ , my country, please have (2) _____ in me. And I will, my team will finish this mission."

Helped by handle bars installed on the outer body of this spacecraft, he is now moving. The flag of PRC is on (3) _____ by one astronaut, with the background of the earth. We can see the flag. He is (4) _____ the flag, the flag of PRC, for the first time being on float by an astronaut.

Well, all the activities outside this spacecraft has been finished at this (5) _____ . And now they are about to get back to the module, (6) _____ they have already return to the module, (7) _____

_____

Directions: *In this part, you are going to watch a video clip. When you watch the video for the first time, you should pay attention to its main idea and answer some general comprehension questions. When the clip is played for the second time, you should focus on important details and answer some specific comprehension questions. When the conversation is repeated for the third and fourth time, you should complete the sentences with the words or phrases you have heard in the news.*

Glossary

(1) parachute *n.* 降落伞   (4) muscle *n.* 肌肉

(2) reentry module 返回舱   (5) shield *v.* 防护

(3) helicopter *n.* 直升飞机   (6) accommodation *n.* 住所,舱位

Task 1

👁 *Now watch the video for the first time and answer questions 1 to 2.*

(1) What is this clip mainly about?

    A. It is about the landing of the Shenzhou Ⅶ.

    B. It is about the interview of the three astronauts.

    C. It tells us what work should be done for the astronauts after landing.

    D. It tells us the hard work of the ground crew.

(2) Why is it difficult for astronauts to be out of the module?

    A. Something wrong with their muscle.

    B. They have high blood pressure.

    C. They are lack of the weight.

    D. They have to get used to the gravity of the earth.

Task 2

👁 *Now watch the video for the second time and answer questions 3 to 5.*

(3) When the spacecraft landed, who went to help astronauts out of the module?

    A. Pilot of helicopter.

    B. Scientists.

    C. Ground crew.

    D. Physiologist.

(4) What is the biggest physiological difficulty at that moment?

    A. The health for reentry module next time.

    B. The weightlessness after the flying mission.

    C. The flexibility of their limbs in mission.

    D. The distribution of blood in their body.

(5) What happened first after they were out of the module?

    A. They received flowers sent by the ground crew.

    B. They just sat in the chair and did nothing.

    C. They received the interview of the reporter.

    D. They took pictures with the reporter.

Task 3

👁 *Now watch the video twice and complete the sentences by filling in the blanks numbered 1 to 7 with the words and phrases you have just heard in the news. At the end of this task, there will be a pause for you to check what you've written.*

(1) We have seen the main parachute has been _____.

(2) So it means the helicopter is _____ this spacecraft.

(3) The biggest _____ difficulty at the moment is simply the distribution of blood in the body.

(4) Because the blood system has been working in the _____ environment for quite some time.

(5) They are making way for the astronauts to get out of the _____.

(6) With the mission _____,—job well done, and they are receiving flowers sent by the ground crew.

(7) We've gone through some experiments and testing and medical _____.

Listening Skills

Listening comprehensive practice (2)

1. Dictation

Directions: *Listen to the following passage. Altogether the passage will be read to you four times. During the first reading, which will be read at normal speed, listen and try to understand the meaning. For the second and third readings, the passage will be read sentence by sentence, or phrase by phrase, with intervals of 15 seconds. The last reading will be read at normal speed again and during this time you should check your work. You will then be given 2 minutes to check through your work once more.*

_____

_____

_____

_____

_____

2. Fill in the blanks

Directions: *Listen to the following listening material and fill in the blanks with exact words or phrases you have just heard.*

(1)

A bomb attack in the CI religious center in Baghdad on Friday killed 10 people; more than 20 other were injured. The leader of the religious center _____ the group ∗∗∗ in _____ for the attack. But an American army general _____ security in Baghdad says the level of _____ has decreased since new security measures began earlier this week. In the separate incident the United States military said one _____ soldier was killed in an attack on the security stop southwest of ∗∗∗∗. A _____ said the officials are searching for two other solders who are reportedly missing after the attack.

(2)

The President of Iran says the country has successfully _____ the _____ for the first time. The announcement is likely to increase _____ of Iran's nuclear program as U. N _____ approaches for Iran to end the nuclear fueling enrichment. VOA _____ Charles Mick Dona has more from Middle East _____ and _____.

(3)

Such a feeling is coming over me, there is _____ in most everything I see. Not a cloud in the sky got the sun in my _____, and I won't be surprised if it's a dream. Everything I want the world to be is now coming true _____ for me. And the _____ is clear, it is because you are here. You are the nearest thing to _____ that I have seen. I am on the top of the world, down on _____ and the only explanation I can find is the love that I've found, ever since you have been around, your love put me at the top of the world. Something in the wind had learned my name, and it is telling me that things are not the same in the _____ on the trees and the touch of the _____, there is a pleas incense of happiness for me. There is only one wish on my mind, when this day is _____ I hope that I will find that tomorrow will be just same for you and me, all I need will be _____ if you are here.

3. Answer the questions

Directions: *Listen to the news and write down the main idea in your own words.*

News 1

(1) What should Iran seriously consider?

_____

_____

_____

(2) At what occasion did he say so?

_____

_____

_____

News 2

(1) What did the United States warn?

_____

_____

_____

(2) What did the United States urge the nearby countries to do?

_____

_____

_____

PART TWO
Viewing and Speaking

I

Preview Exercises

1. Please watch the following two clips and tell us how many ways of greetings and introduction according to your knowledge.

> Hello (Hi).
> Nice to meet you.
> Pleased to meet you.
> It's my pleasure to meet you.
> This is…
> I'm…
> You can call me...
> I work in…

2. Please say hello to your new classmates and introduce yourself.

II

Warming up Exercises

1. Please watch the following clips and tell us kinds of greetings and introductions in our daily life.

2. Please introduce yourself to us in front of the classroom.

3. Do the presentation in different situations.

Listening Material Review

Directions: *In this section, you are going to listen to the material which you have heard in lis-*
tening course again for several times. After finishing the first – time listening, you
have to tell us what you have learned. After finishing the second – time listening,
you should focus on important details and answer some specific questions in your
own words. When it is played for the third and the fourth time, you should tell us
what you think of this clip. And at last you are required to listen and repeat several
sentences in the clip.

Task 1

◁ *Questions for the first-time listening.*

What is the relationship between the man and woman? And why?

_____

Task 2

◁ *Questions for the second-time listening.*

(1) Is the woman's family big? And why?

_____

(2) What does "personal information" include ?

_____

(3) Do you think whether the woman has a job or not?

_____

Task 3

◁ *Questions for the third and the fourth-time listening.*

(1) What do you think of the woman?

_____

_____

(2) Retell the conversation you have just heard.

_____

_____

_____

_____

Task 4

 Now listen to the following sentences twice and repeat the whole sentences after you hear the sound of bell.

(1) _____

(2) _____

(3) _____

(4) _____

IV   Video-aural Material Review

Directions: *In this section, you are going to watch the video clip which you have done in listening course. After watching it for the first time, you have to tell us what you have learned. When you watch for the second time, you should focus on important details and answer some specific questions in your own words. When it is played for the third and the fourth time, you should tell us what you think of this clip. And at last you are required to listen to and repeat several sentences in the clip.*

Task 1

Questions for the first-time watching.

Why are they greeting so frequently in the morning?

_____

Task 2

Questions for the second-time watching.

(1) What is Jack doing?

_____

(2) Who will be the host ? Can you tell the reason?

_____

(3) Do you know the name of the TV station? How do you know it?

_____

Task 3

Questions for the third and the fourth-time watching.

(1) What do you think of would-be hosts?

_____

_____

(2) Retell the clip you have just watched.

_____

_____

_____

_____

Task 4

Now listen to the following sentences twice and repeat the whole sentences after you hear the sound of bell.

(1) _____

(2) _____

(3) _____

(4) _____

Ⅴ Additional Video-aural Material

Directions: *In this section, you are going to watch an additional video clip. After watching it for the first time, you have to tell us what you have learned. When you watch for the second time, you should focus on important details and answer some specific questions in your own words. When it is played for the third and the fourth time, you should tell us what you think of this clip. And at last you are required to listen to and repeat several sentences in the clip.*

Task 1

👁 *Questions for the first-time watching.*

What are Bob and Jennifer going to do?

_____

Task 2

👁 *Questions for the second-time watching.*

(1) Do they find the right place? Why?

_____

(2) What kind of activity is it?

_____

(3) Do they finally find the right person?

_____

Questions for the third and fourth-time watching.

(1) What's wrong with Bob and Jennifer?

_____

_____

(2) Retell the clip you have just watched.

_____

_____

_____

_____

Task 4

Now listen to the following sentences twice and repeat the whole sentences after you hear the sound of bell.

(1) _____

(2) _____

(3) _____

(4) _____

VI   Phonetics Tips

The Correct Pronunciation of English Alphabets

1. Do you know how to pronounce English Alphabets correctly? Try to read the following letters.

A	B	C	D	E	F	G	H	I	J	K	L	M
/ei/	/bi/	/si/	/di/	/i:/	/ef/	/dʒi:/	/eitʃ/	/ai/	/dʒei/	/kei/	/el/	/em/
N	O	P	Q	R	S	T	U	V	W	X	Y	Z
/en/	/əu/	/pi:/	/kju:/	/a:/	/es/	/ti:/	/ju:/	/vi:/	/dʌblju:/	/eks/	/wai/	/zi:/ /zed/

2. How to pronounce the letters when they are in different words? Please look at the following charts:

Single letters 单个字母

A	/ei/ name cake table /æ/ apple cat map am /ɑː/ want dance /ɔ/ what watch	N	/n/ no know new hand
B	/b/ book big bag box	O	/əu/ old home nose coke /ɔ/ dog not clock box
C	/k/ cat cake cup clock car /s/ face nice pencil	P	/p/ map jeep pig pen apple
D	/d/ desk doll dog dad	Q	/kw/ quite quilt quick
E	/iː/ he she meet me /e/ elephant egg bed pen	R	/r/ red radio brother racket
F	/f/ fine friend fly foot fan	S	/s/ sit miss this smile books /z/ nose those rose rulers
G	/g/ gun glass glad glove	T	/t/ it sit not that table little
H	/h/ hat he house hand	U	/juː/ use usually excuse /ʌ/ bus us sun duck /u/ put pull push
I	/ai/ fine bike five ice /i/ is sit miss pig picture	V	/v/ five vase very seven
J	/dʒ/ jeep jam jacket jar	W	/w/ we window watch want
K	/k/ kite cake black thank	X	/ks/ box six fox
L	/l/ leg left ruler flag lamp	Y	/ai/ my fly why bye /j/ yes yellow /i/ happy baby very
M	/m/ am map my mouth milk	Z	/z/ zoo zero

Vowel clusters 元音组合

ai	/ei/ wait paint		ir	/ə:/ bird girl shirt thirty
ay	/ei/ may play day say		oa	/əu/ boat coat
air	/eə/ air hair chair		ong	/ɔŋ/ long song
al	/ɔ:/ tall small ball		oo	/u/ book foot good /u:/ moon balloon
ar	/ɑ:/ farther car arm		or	/ɔ:/ short fork port /ə:/ word world work
ea	/i:/ meat tea read /e/ head bread ready /iə/ theater /iə/ ear hear near		oor	/ɔ:/ door floor
-ear	/eə/ bear /ə:/ earth		ore	/ɔ:/ more store sore
ee	/i:/ meet see feet jeep		ou	/au/ out house mouth
eir	/eə/ their		our	/ɔ:/ four your /auə/ our
er	/ə/ worker teacher /ə:/ her		oy	/ɔi/ boy toy
ere	/iə/ here /eə/ where there		ow	/əu/ bowl window /au/ now cow flower
ew	/ju:/ new few /u:/ flew grew		ur	/ə:/ turn
igh	/ai/ right high bright			

Consonant clusters 辅音组合

th	/θ/ thank mouth /ð/ this that with	ch	/tʃ/ child chair catch /k/ school Christmas / dʒ/ sandwich
tr	/tr/ tree train truck	wh	/w/ white wheel what /h/ who whose whom
dr	/dr/ dress driver	ts	/ts/ jackets kites
sh	/ʃ/ shirt wash short	ds	/dz/ birds friends
tw	/tw/ two twin twenty		

I

Preview Exercises

1. Please watch the following clip and tell us what happens on the woman teacher. Fill in the blanks according to your understanding of the clip.

When the new_____comes, the_____
play a practical_____on her. How_____
She is!

2. What do you think of using mobile phones in the classroom?

II

Warming up Exercises

Please watch the following clip and answer the following questions:

1. What is your first impression about the pretty woman in the movie?
2. How can you get that impression about her?
3. Can you list the phenomenon of bad manners and good manners?
4. Check the preview exercises.

Listening Material Review

Directions: *In this section, you are going to listen to the program which you have heard in lis-*
tening course again for several times. After finishing the first – time listening, you
have to tell us what you have learned. After finishing the second – time listening,
you should focus on important details and answer some specific questions in your
own words. When it is played for the third and the fourth time, you should tell us
what you think of this program. And at last you are required to listen and repeat
several sentences in the program.

Task 1

Questions for the first-time listening.

What does the program tell us?

_____

Task 2

Questions for the second-time listening.

(1) Can you list some table manners mentioned in this program?

_____

(2) Can you tell us more about the table manners you know?

_____

(3) What if you confuse to use the forks?

_____

Task 3

 Questions for the third and the fourth-time listening.

(1) Tell us some the good table manners in China.

_____

_____

(2) Retell the conversation you have just heard.

_____

_____

_____

_____

Task 4

Now listen to the following sentences twice and repeat the whole sentences after you hear the sound of bell.

(1) _____

(2) _____

(3) _____

(4) _____

IV   Video-aural Material Review

Directions: *In this section, you are going to watch the video clip which you have done in listening course. After watching it for the first time, you have to tell us what you have learned. When you watch for the second time, you should focus on important details and answer some specific questions in your own words. When it is played for the third and the fourth time, you should tell us what you think of this clip. And at last you are required to listen to and repeat several sentences in the clip.*

Task 1

👁 *Questions for the first-time watching.*

Who is this program most probably for?

_____

Task 2

👁 *Questions for the second-time watching.*

(1) How will you give an order according to this clip?

_____

(2) What should children do when they finish eating?

_____

(3) What is procedure of eating in a restaurant?

_____

Task 3

👁 *Questions for the third and fourth-time watching.*

(1) What kind of program is it?

_____

_____

(2) Retell the clip you have just watched.

_____

_____

_____

_____

Task 4

*Now listen to the following sentences twice and repeat the whole sentences after you hear the sound of bell.*

(1) _____

(2) _____

(3) _____

(4) _____

V   Additional Video-aural Material

Directions: *In this section, you are going to watch an additional video clip. After watching it for the first time, you have to tell us what you have learned. When you watch for the second time, you should focus on important details and answer some specific questions in your own words. When it is played for the third and the fourth time, you should tell us what you think of this clip. And at last you are required to listen to and repeat several sentences in the clip.*

Glossary

(1) resume *n.* 简历，履历	(3) suite *n.* 一批；一套；组；套
(2) flawless *adj.* 完美的，无瑕的	(4) tude *n.* 花花公子

Task 1

👁 *Questions for the first-time watching.*

What can we learn from this clip?

Task 2

👁 *Questions for the second-time watching.*

(1) What are the good manners in job-hunting mentioned in this clip?

(2) What does "punctual" mean?

(3) Why should a "thank-you letter" be written?

Task 3

👁 *Questions for the third and fourth-time watching.*

(1) Do you have the experience of interview?

(2) Retell the clip you have just watched.

🔊 *Now listen to the following sentences twice and repeat the whole sentences after you hear the sound of bell.*

(1) _____

(2) _____

(3) _____

(4) _____

VI   **Phonetics Tips**

Consonants:

What is a consonant?

> *Consonants are made by stopping the airflow in your mouth, either partially or completely. There are 24 consonants in English.*

Stops: [p]—[b], [t]—[d], [k]—[g]

Directions: The stop consonants are made by completely stopping the airflow in the mouth, and then releasing the airflow into the sounds. There are six stops in English: [p]—[b], [t]—[d], [k]—[g]. [p] [t] [k] are voiceless stops because they are not accompanied by vibration from the larynx , while the [b] [d] [g] are voiced stips.

[p]—[b]	1. 双唇紧闭，憋住气，然后突然张开，使气流冲出口腔，发出爆破的声音。 2. [p]是清辅音，只送气，声带不振动；[b]是浊辅音，声带振动。
[t]—[d]	1. 舌尖紧贴上齿龈憋住气，然后突然张开，使气流冲出口腔，发出爆破的声音。 2. [t]是清辅音，只送气，声带不振动；[d]是浊辅音，声带振动。

148

[k]—[g]

| 1. | 舌后部隆起紧贴软腭，憋住气，然后突然张开使气流冲出口腔，发出爆破的声音。 |
| 2. | [k]是清辅音，只送气，声带不振动；[g]是浊辅音，声带振动。 |

Exercises：

1. Words

peak—beak	tip—dip	Kate—gate
pack—back	tan—Dan	tuck—tug
cap—cab	toe – doe	bicker – bigger
napped – napped	bet – bed	crime – grim

2. Phrases

paint an apple	lift it	a black cat
paper sheep	time and tide	keep quiet
a big box	do a good job	the game of guess
the best book	a double bed	suger and cigarettes

3. Sentences

There are two pens and three pencils in the pencil box.

He bought a better bag.

Time runs too fast.

Dad didn't want to see the doctor.

He looks quite sick back from UK.

He got his degree in a big university.

4. Tongue twisters

Peter Piper picked a peck of pickled peppers.

"Betty Botter had some butter, but," she said, "this butter's bitter. If I bake this bitter butter, it would make my batter bitter. But a bit of better butter-that would make my batter better."

The students are talking about the mid-term tests.

David visited me the day before yesterday.

The kids killed the duck and took it to the kitchen.

The great Greek grape growers grow great Greek Grapes.

Fricatives（1）：[f]—[v],[s]—[z],[h]

Directions：If the strips completely block the air stream for a time in the pronunciation, the fricatives only partially block it, thus causing the friction—like noise characteristic of there sounds. There are nine fricatives in English.

[f]—[v]	1. 下唇（指下唇靠里约 1/3 的部位）轻触上齿，气流由唇齿间的缝隙中通过，摩擦成音。 2. [f]是清辅音，发音时送气强，但声带不振动；[v]是浊辅音，发音时声带振动，气流较弱。
[s]—[z]	1. 舌端靠近齿龈，气流由舌前端齿龈所形成的窄缝中通过时摩擦成音。 2. [s]是清辅音，发音时要送气，但声带不振动；[z]是浊辅音，发音时声带振动，不送气。
[h]	1. 气流自由溢出口腔，只在通过声门时发生轻微的摩擦。 2. 口形不定，随后面的原因而变化。 3. 声带不振动，是个清辅音。

Exercises：

1. Words

fast—vast	sip—zip	hug—heal
few—view	racer—razor	who—whole
leaf—leave	spice—spies	hair—half
safe—save	bussing—buzzing	house—human

2. Phrases

very fast	a soft voice	happy home
very safe	the Sound of Music	hack hammer
five – thieves	those beautiful roses	her hair
a beautiful view	lost his keys	whose hat

3. Sentences

Phillip is fat and foolish.

Frank saved Vicki's life in 1954.

Cindy collects all types of stamps.

The sun rises in the east and sets in the west.

He had a bad habit.

He did his homework in a hurry.

4. Tongue twisters

A flee and a fly were trapped in a flute, and they tried to flee for their lives.

I have never driven to the valley to have a vacation.

Her sister is in Class Six.

Lizzie has the zest to see the zebras in the zoo.

Who cut her husband's hair?

I Preview Exercises

1. Here are some pictures of some famous people. Can you tell us what these people are and the achievements they have made?
2. Do you think they are full of confidence and can you describe their facial expression for us?

> They are _____and they are famous for/ gain great fame in/enjoy good reputation in_____.

> I can find/see/trace _____in their face/gestures.

3. Please find out some more ways of expressing your ideas.

II Warming up Exercises

Questions:

1. The above pictures were taken from the 2004 and 2008 Olympic Games. Can you describe the person in each picture for me and can you tell us what happened to them at that special moment?

2. When you are successful, it is very easy to be confident. Is it possible to be confident when you fail?

3. How to rebuild your confidence when you are down?

Listening Material Review

Directions: After finishing the first-time listening, you have to tell us what you have learned. After finishing the second-time listening, you should focus on important details and answer some specific questions in your own words. When it is played for the third and the fourth time, you should tell us what you think of this material. And at last you are required to listen and repeat several sentences in the material.

Task 1

Questions for the first-time listening.

What is this material meaning about?

_____

Task 2

Questions for the second-time listening.

(1) Can you tell me the meaning of *dress well*?

_____

(2) Can you tell the meaning of *gossip* and give one example to prove your idea?

_____

(3) What are the advantages of speaking up?

_____

Questions for the third and fourth-time listening.

(1) What do you think of this clip? Can you list more ways to make us confident?

_____

_____

(2) Can you retell the main idea of the material in your own words?

_____

Task 4

Now listen to the following sentences twice and repeat the whole sentences after you hear the sound of bell.

(1) _____

(2) _____

(3) _____

(4) _____

IV   Video-aural Material Review

Directions: In this section, you are going to watch the video clip which you have done in listening course. After watching it for the first time, you have to tell us what you have learned. When you watch for the second time, you should focus on important details and answer some specific questions in your own words. When it is played for the third and the fourth time, you should tell us what you think of this clip. And at last you are required to listen to and repeat several sentences in the clip.

Task 1

👁 *Questions for the first-time watching.*

What is this clip meaning about?

_____

Task 2

👁 *Questions for the second-time watching*

(1) Why should we love our self?

_____

(2) How to talk to yourself?

_____

(3) How to make yourself feel good?

_____

Task 3

👁 *Questions for the third and fourth-time watching.*

(1) What do you think of this clip?

_____

_____

(2) Retell the message you have just watched.

_____

_____

_____

_____

Task 4

🔊 *Now listen to the following sentences twice and repeat the whole sentences after you hear the sound of bell.*

(1) _____

(2) _____

(3) _____

(4) _____

V   Additional Video-aural Material

Directions: In this section, you are going to watch an additional video clip. After watching it for the first time, you have to tell us what you have learned. When you watch for the second time, you should focus on the important details and answer some specific questions in your own words. When it is played for the third and the fourth time, you should tell us what you think of this clip. And at last you are required to listen to and repeat several sentences in the clip.

（1）pantsuit *n.* 长裤与衣相配成套的便服　　（8）senator *n.* 参议员

（2）profoundly *adv.* 深深地　　（9）downstate *n.* 在州里的南部

（3）worthy *adj.* 有价值的,可尊敬的,值得的

（4）upstate *n.* 远离大城市或离海岸较远的地方

（5）Pinders Corner 频德角(地名,位于纽约)

（6）Liz Moynihan 丽兹·莫伊尼汉(人名)

（7）Daniel Patrick Moynihan 丹尼尔·帕特里克·莫伊尼汉(人名)

Task 1

👁 *Questions for the first-time watching.*

Who is the woman speaker in the video and what is this clip meaning about?

_____

Task 2

👁 *Questions for the second-time watching.*

（1）How long did this election last and how many debates did she take part in?

_____

（2）What were the people discussing with Hillary?

_____

（3）Why did she express her appreciation to the audience?

_____

Task 3

👁 *Questions for the third and fourth-time watching.*

（1）What do you think of this clip?

_____

_____

（2）Retell the message you have just watched.

_____

_____

Task 4

 Now listen to the following sentences twice and repeat the whole sentences after you hear the sound of bell.

(1) _____

(2) _____

(3) _____

(4) _____

VI　Phonetics Tips

Consonants：

Fricatives（2）：[θ]—[ð], [ʃ]—[ʒ]

[θ]—[ð]	1. 舌尖轻触上齿下面的边缘, 气流由舌齿间的窄缝泄出, 摩擦成音。 2. [θ]是清辅音, 发音时送气强, 但声带不振动；[ð]是浊辅音, 发音时声带振动, 送气弱。
[ʃ]—[ʒ]	1. 舌端(包括舌尖)抬起, 靠近齿龈后部(但不要贴住), 舌前也随之向硬腭抬起, 形成一条狭长的通道, 气流通过时摩擦成音。双唇稍须向前突出并稍收圆。 2. [ʃ]是清辅音, 发音时要送气, 但声带不振动；[ʒ]是浊辅音, 发音时声带振动, 不送气。

Exercises:

1. Words

   sick—thick   sheep—jeep

   sigh—sign   shine—sigh

   doze—those   shoes—chose

   closing—clothing   pressure—pleasure

   pass—path   fission—vision

2. Phrases

   a thousand thanks   a fashion show

   a wealthy mother   push the bush

   a healthy father   special fish

   through thick and thin   Shirley's shoes

   the theme of the thesis   shrink shorts

3. Sentences

   Together they went through thick and thin .

   Something is better than nothing.

   Mr. Smith used to be healthy and wealthy.

   Their father is taller than any of them.

   It is shiny today. Let's go fishing.

   Don't mention that special shop again.

   She usually gives me a massage while watching television.

   He went with pleasure to the university of great prestige.

4. Tongue twisters

   A: I can think of six thin things.

   B: Six thin things, can you?

   A: Yes, I can think of six thin things.

   B: And of six thick things, too.

   If a shipshape shop stocks six shipshape shop – soiled ships, how many shipshape shop –
   soiled ships would six shipshape ship shops stock?

Eat at pleasure, drink with measure.

Affricates: [tʃ] — [dʒ]

Direction: [tʃ] and [dʒ] are affricate sounds, produced by blocking off the breath – stream between the tongue and gum ridge, for stop and a fricative. The term affricate means "blend", in this case, consisting of a stop and a fricative. The [tʃ] is a blend combined of [t] and [ʃ], while the [dʒ] is a blend of [d] and [ʒ].

[tʃ]—[dʒ]

1. 先将舌端贴住上齿龈,舌两侧向上翘起贴住两边上齿的底部,憋住气,然后让气流从舌端与上齿龈间强烈摩擦而出。
2. /tʃ/是清辅音,发音时要送气,但声带不振动;/dʒ/是浊辅音,发音时声带振动,不送气。

Exercises:

1. Words

    chest—jest   cheer—jeer
    choke—joke   chump—jump
    etch—edge   searches—surges
    riches—ridges   lunched—lunged
    batches—badges   perched—purged

2. Phrases

    chage the chamber   June and July
    catch the chap   a jor of jam
    chase the charming girl   orange juice

3. Sentences

    This match is both a chance and a challenge.
    The teacher is writing on the blackboard with chalk.
    He sat in the chair watching the beautiful china without lunch.

Tom was just joking with Jack.

The majority of the students like orange juice.

The joyous judge made a just judgment.

4. Tongue twisters

The French teacher is watching the Chinese children play.

Jack is joking with George in a Japanese jail.

5. Dialogue

A: How are the children doing in your class?

B: They're all doing fine. Let me show you some of their pictures.

A: Which child is this?

B: That's Charles.

A: What a large child!

B: All my children are large.

A: And which child is this?

B: That's James.

A: What an agile child.

B: All my children are agile.

A: Now which child is this?

B: That's Joanna. Joanna hopes to go to college.

A: "All my children hope to go to college." Right?

I

Preview Exercises

1. In listening course, we have heard a talk which discusses difficulties of Chinese people. Please describe the pictures below with what you have heard in your listening class.

People in Wenchuan, Sichuan
_____ on May. 12 in
the year of 2008. But people
there have never given up.

_____ from across the country
_____ to help hurricane victims.

After _____ our economy from a
recession, _____
are creating jobs again.

2. What is the Chinese people attitude toward such disasters?

_____

Warming up Exercises

1. Look at the pictures given below and read the words in the box.

The picture describes _____.

The picture describes

_____.

2. Describe your family within language tips as follows.

"I love my family because they make me feel warm. I thank my parents who support me when I decide to do something.

I love my grandfather because he tells me interesting stories."

3. **The pictures above describe the friendly relation between teacher and students as well as amongst colleagues. We depend on them emotionally. Practice it with your partners.**

III Listening Material Review

Directions: *In this section, you are going to listen to the material which you have heard in listening course again for several times. After finishing the first-time listening, you have to tell us what you have learned. After finishing the second-time listening, you should focus on important details and answer some specific questions in your own words. When it is played for the third and the fourth time, you should tell us what you think of this material. And at last you are required to listen and repeat several sentences in the material.*

Task 1

Questions for the first-time listening.

What is the main idea of this passage?

_____

Task 2

Questions for the second-time listening.

(1) Did the young girl help the little boy Howard Kelly?

_____

(2) Did the boy become a doctor later?

_____

(3) Did the girl recover from the illness?

_____

Task 3

Questions for the third and fourth-time listening.

(1) Did the girl have enough money to pay?

_____

(2) Why did the boy help the girl?

_____

_____

Task 4

 Now listen to the following sentences twice and repeat the four sentences.

(1) _____

(2) _____

(3) _____

(4) _____

IV Video-aural Material Review

Directions: *In this section, you are going to watch the video clip which you have done in lis-*
tening course. After watching it for the first time, you have to tell us what you
have learned. When you watch for the second time, you should focus on important
details and answer some specific questions in your own words. When it is played for
the third and the fourth time, you should tell us what you think of this clip. And
at last you are required to listen to and repeat several sentences in the clip.

Task 1

Questions for the first-time watching.

 Did the students like Mr. Keating's course?

_____

Task 2

👁️ *Questions for the second-time watching.*

(1) Did the student in the episode complete the task his teacher asked?

_____

(2) Could you repeat the sentence the teacher says when he finds the student sitting with worry?

_____

(3) The student, Todd, worked out a metaphor when he mentioned truth. What is it? How does the metaphor work?

_____

Task 3

👁️ *Questions for the third and fourth-time watching.*

(1) The teacher encouraged the student to work out a poem. Can you still remember any sentences in his poem? Repeat them as much as possible.

_____

(2) How will the student express his appreciation?

_____

Task 4

🔊 *Now listen to the following sentences twice and repeat them.*

(1) _____

(2) _____

(3) _____

(4) _____

V Additional Video-aural Material

Directions: In this section, you are going to watch an additional video clip. After watching it for the first time, you have to tell us what you have learned. When you watch for the second time, you should focus on important details and answer some specific questions in your own words. When it is played for the third and the fourth time, you should tell us what you think of this clip. And at last you are required to listen to and repeat several sentences in the clip.

Task 1

👁 *Questions for the first-time watching.*

How did the father express when he found his son need more food?

_____

Task 2

👁 *Questions for the second-time watching.*

(1) How did the father express when he found his son does not need food any more?

_____

(2) Where did the family live in?

_____

(3) How do you view this family? Do you think a kid would be happy and satisfied when she/he lives in such a family?

_____

Task 3

👁 *Questions for the third and fourth-time watching.*

(1) How many persons in their family? And who were they?

_____

(2) Where did their parents (grand – parents) live in?

_____

Task 4

 Now listen to the following sentences twice and repeat the whole.

(1) _____

(2) _____

(3) _____

(4) _____

VI   Phonetics Tips

Consonants

Nasals：[m]，[n]，[ŋ]

Directions：*Unlike stops，or any other sound in the language，there is an opening into the nasal cavity so that the sound can be resonated through the nose.*

[m]	1. 发鼻辅音[m]时双唇闭拢，软腭下垂，气流从鼻腔泄出。 2. 是浊辅音，发音时声带振动。
[n]	1. 发鼻辅音时舌尖紧贴上齿龈，形成阻碍，软腭下垂，气流从鼻腔泄出。 2. [n]也是浊辅音，发音时声带振动。
[ŋ]	1. 鼻辅音的发音部位和[k][g]相同。即舌后抬起贴住软腭，但发时软腭需下垂，以打开鼻腔通道，使气流从鼻腔泄出。 2. [ŋ]同样是浊辅音，发音时声带振动。

Exercises:

1. Words

   Kim—kin—king   whim—win—wing

   some—son—sung   dumb—done—dung

   rum—ran—rung   whims—whins—wings

   ram—ran—rang   pam—pan—pang

   Tim—tin—ting   stum—stun—stung

2. Phrases

   Tom's room   a fine needle   a long string

   a warm home   a nice tune   a strong drink

   on the moon   seven lonely nights   a young singer

   the sun and the moon   a friend in need   the English language

3. Sentences

   Come on, it's time for home.

   Come and meet Mary and James.

   The more, the merrier.

   Time means money.

   I don't know his name.

   My aunt gave me those knives.

   We'll finish this lesson soon.

   No news is good news.

   This morning they were singing the same song.

   Things are getting wrong.

   When the spring is coming, birds begin singing.

4. Tongue twisters

   A monk's monkey mounted a monastery wall munching mashed melon and

   melted macaroni.

   The woman's husband is ninety-nine years old.

   Ding-dong, ting a ling!

   What do you bring?

I

Preview Exercises

1. **Please list some names of the buildings or places in the University and try to practice the following sentences and expressions.**

Could you tell me where _____ is?

Do you think you could tell me where _____ is?

I wonder if you could tell me how to get to _____.

Excuse me, would you mind answering a few questions?

May I ask you a few questions?

2. **Please list different ways of requesting information.**

II

Warming up Exercises

1. **Suppose you are on the campus and you meet a foreign teacher. He asks you some questions. Please make dialogues by using expressions of asking for and giving information.**

2. Please give some words related to the following items.

Grade	
Majors	
Courses	
Degree	

3. Make dialogue with your partner discussing about the courses in college.

Listening Material Review

Directions: *In this section, you are going to listen to the material which you have heard in listening course again for several times. After finishing the first-time listening, you have to tell us what you have learned. After finishing the second-time listening, you should focus on important details and answer some specific questions in your own words. When it is played for the third and the fourth time, you should tell us what you think of this material. And at last you are required to listen and repeat several sentences in thematerial.*

Task 1

◁ *Questions for the first-time listening.*

What is this material about?

Questions for the second-time listening.

(1) What does PhD refer to?

_____ .

(2) Can you catch the meaning of the word M. D. ?

_____ .

(3) From which countries did the students who got one-third of the doctorates in the U. S. come? And what are they chiefly majoring in?

_____ .

Task 3

Questions for the third and the fourth-time listening.

(1) Summarize the main idea of the report and retell it in your own words.

_____ .

(2) Why do you choose English as your major?

_____

_____

_____

Task 4

Now listen to the following sentences twice and repeat the whole sentences after you hear the sound of bell.

(1) _____ .

(2) _____ .

(3) _____ .

(4) _____ .

IV   Video-aural Material Review

Directions: *In this section, you are going to watch the video clip which you have done in listening course. After watching it for the first time, you have to tell us what you have learned. When you watch for the second time, you should focus on important details and answer some specific questions in your own words. When it is played for the third and the fourth time, you should tell us what you think of this clip. And at last you are required to listen to and repeat several sentences in the clip.*

Task 1

👁 *Questions for the first-time watching.*

What is this clip about?

_____

Task 2

👁 *Questions for the second-time watching.*

(1) What does the sentence "I was just wondering" mean?

_____

(2) Can you catch the meaning of the word/phrase " here it goes " ?

_____

(3) What does the sentence " P. S. I would've said 'keep in touch', but unfortunately we never were in touch. " mean?

_____

Task 3

👁 *Questions for the third and the fourth-time watching.*

(1) Retell what you have watched.

_____

_____

_____

(2) What were you thinking about when you gradated from high school?

_____

_____

_____

Task 4

 Now listen to the following sentences twice and repeat the whole sentences after you hear the sound of bell.

(1) _____

(2) _____

(3) _____

(4) _____

V   Additional Video-aural Material

Directions: *In this section, you are going to watch an additional video clip. After watching it for the first time, you have to tell us what you have learned. When you watch for the second time, you should focus on important details and answer some specific questions in your own words. When it is played for the third and the fourth time, you should tell us what you think of this clip. And at last you are required to listen to and repeat several sentences in the clip.*

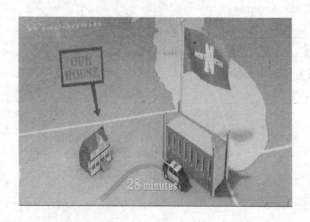

Task 1

👁 *Questions for the first-time watching.*

What is this clip talking about?

_____

Task 2

👁 *Questions for the second-time watching.*

(1) What does the phrase "college application season" mean?

_____

(2) Can you catch the meaning of the word " academics " ?

_____

(3) What does the sentence "you can never start a plan too early" mean according to the speaker?

_____

Task 3

👁 *Questions for the third and fourth-time watching.*

(1) What do you think of this clip?

_____

_____

(2) Describe what you have just watched in your own words.

_____

_____

_____

Task 4

🔊 *Now listen to the following sentences twice and repeat the whole sentences after you hear the sound of bell.*

(1) _____

(2) _____

(3) _____

(4) _____

Phonetics Tips

Consonants

Approximants and Lateral：[w]，[j]，[r]，[l]

Directions：[w]，[j]，[r] *are called approximants because it is an articulation in which the articulators approach each other but do not get sufficiently close to each other to produce a complete consonant.* [w] *and* [j] *are also called semivowels.* [l] *is called a lateral because during its pronunciation, the passage of air through the mouth does not go in the usual way along the centre of the tongue.*

[w]

> 1. 发半元音[w]时舌后部向硬腭抬起,舌位很高,和[u:]相似。双唇需收圆、收小并稍向前突出。
> 2. [w]是浊辅音,发音时声带应振动。

[j]

> 1. 发半元音[j]时舌前部向硬腭高高抬起,和[i:]相似。双唇向两旁伸展成扁平形,口形也和[i:]相同。
> 2. [j]也是一个浊辅音,发音时声带振动。

[r]

> 1. 发[r]时舌头卷起,靠近(不是贴近)上齿龈后部。舌的两侧稍收拢,轻触上齿龈的两侧,双唇突出并收圆。
> 2. [r]是个浊辅音,发音时声带振动。

[l]

> 1. 清晰舌侧音:舌尖及舌端紧贴上齿龈,舌前向硬腭抬起,气流从舌的旁边(一侧或两侧)泄出。
> 2. 含糊舌侧音:舌端紧贴上齿龈,舌前下陷,舌后上台,舌面形成凹形,气流在此凹槽中产生共鸣。
> 3. [l]是浊辅音,发音时声带振动。

Exercises:

1. Words

where	yeild	radio	lawn
word	yellow	rival	leave
wait	youth	writer	fluent
sweet	beauty	arrive	flight
swim	stupid	great	bottle
request	opinion	writer	cattle

2. Phrases

White Swan Hotel   worry about the road

wake up your wife   raise the rock

a beautiful excuse   long-lasting

a humorous refusal   a little lab

new value   last mail

3. Sentences

Where there's a will, there is a way.

What a wonderful wedding it was.

You will soon get used to the new youngster.

Your computer is of great value.

When in Rome, do as the Romans do.

We have fresh bread for breakfast.

Live and learn.

Like father, like son.

Let sleeping dogs lie.

4. Tongue twisters

How much wood would a woodchuck chuck if a woodchuck could chuck wood?

Your new humor is a beautiful excuse.

A tall eastern girl named Short long loved a big Mr Little.

A writer named Wright was instructing his little son how to write Wright right. He said: "It is not right to write Wright as 'rite' —try to write Wright, alright?"

Unit Six Networks

I

Preview Exercises

1. **Please say something about the advantages or disadvantages of networks according to the following pictures.**

This is called _____.
It helps _____.
I like/dislike it because _____.

The reasons why I like … is as follows:
First of all, _____.
Secondly, _____.
Finally, _____.

2. **Please find out some more ways of expressing your attitude toward network, such words as likes, dislikes ,preference.**

Warming up Exercises

1. **Please tell us the advantages and disadvantages of the following pictures referring to the usage of network.**

2. **Summarize your attitude towards network positively or negatively.**

Listening Material Review

Directions: *In this section, you are going to listen to the material which you have heard in listening course again for several times. After finishing the first-time listening, you have to tell us what you have learned. After finishing the second-time listening, you should focus on important details and answer some specific questions in your own words. When it is played for the third and the fourth time, you should tell us what you think of this material. And at last you are required to listen and repeat several sentences in the material.*

Task 1

Questions for the first-time listening.

What is the topic for this clip?

_____

Task 2

Questions for the second-time listening.

(1) Why did John's parents buy a computer to him?

_____

(2) What happened a few months later?

_____

(3) How would they solve this problem?

_____

Task 3

Questions for the third and the fourth-time listening.

(1) What can we learn from the material?

_____

_____

(2) Retell the material you have just heard.

_____

_____

Task 4

 Now listen to the following sentences twice and repeat the whole sentences after you hear the sound of bell.

(1) _____

(2) _____

(3) _____

(4) _____

IV   Video-aural Material Review

Directions: *In this section, you are going to watch the video clip which you have done in listening course. After watching it for the first time, you have to tell us what you have learned. When you watch for the second time, you should focus on important details and answer some specific questions in your own words. When it is played for the third and the fourth time, you should tell us what you think of this clip. And at last you are required to listen to and repeat several sentences in the clip.*

Task 1

Questions for the first-time watching.

What does this clip tell us?

_____

Task 2

Questions for the second-time watching.

(1) What do you understand the glass house?

_____

(2) What is video phone used for?

_____

(3) Do you think ordinary people can go into the space for a visit?

_____

Task 3

Questions for the third and fourth-time watching.

(1) How do computers help do research?

(2) Retell the video clip you have just watched.

Task 4

🔊 *Now listen to the following sentences twice and repeat the whole sentences after you hear the sound of bell.*

(1) _____

(2) _____

(3) _____

(4) _____

V | Additional Video-aural Material

Directions: *In this section, you are going to watch an additional video clip. After watching it for the first time, you have to tell us what you have learned. When you watch for the second time, you should focus on important details and answer some specific questions in your own words. When it is played for the third and the fourth time, you should tell us what you think of this clip. And at last you are required to listen to and repeat several sentences in the clip.*

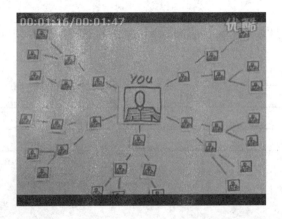

Task 1

👁 *Questions for the first-time watching.*

What does this clip tell us?

_____

Task 2

👁 *Questions for the second-time watching.*

(1) What can we do with the network according to this clip?

_____

(2) Why does network have huge potential?

_____

(3) If you find a person you are interested in, what will you do?

_____

Task 3

👁 *Questions for the third and fourth-time watching.*

(1) Why does it say network is really cool?

_____

_____

(2) Retell the clip you have just watched.

_____

_____

_____

Task 4

🔊 *Now listen to the following sentences twice and repeat the whole sentences after you hear the sound of bell.*

(1) _____

(2) _____

(3) _____

(4) _____

VI Phonetics Tips

Vowels:

What is a vowel?

Vowels are sounds in which there is no obstruction to the flow of an air as it passes from the larynx to the lips. There are 20 vowels in English.

Front vowels and central vowels: [i:]—[i],[e]—[æ];[ə]—[ə:]

[i:]—[i]

> 1. 发前元音[i:]时,舌前部向硬腭抬起,舌位较高,嘴唇向两旁平伸,成微笑状。
> 2. 发前元音[i]时,舌前部也须向硬腭抬起,但舌位比[i:]稍低、稍后。口形扁平,比[i:]稍大。

[e]—[æ]

> 1. 发/e/时舌尖抵下齿,舌前部向硬腭抬起的高度介于[i][æ]之间,牙床半合,唇形中常。
> 2. 发[æ]时舌尖抵下齿,舌身低平。[æ]的舌位在四个前元音中最低。发音时要张大,上下齿之间约可容纳食指和中指。

[ə]—[ə:]

> 1. 英语中[ə]的发音时半张嘴,不圆唇,舌身平放口中,口腔肌肉放松,发短音。
> 2. [ə:]是一个长元音,发音部位与[ə]相同;即舌中部稍隆起。
> 3. [ə]和[ə:]是英语中的中元音。

Exercises:

1. Words

eat—it   bet—bat   sister   shirt
meat—mitt   end—and   afraid   bird

peak—pick   since—sense   together   church
seen—sin   knit—net   famous   earth

2. Phrases
believe in peace   ten pencils   other sisters
leave me alone   the best bed   father and mother
a big city   a mad cat   a nervous worker
give in   a happy man   an early bird

3. Sentences
A friend in need is a friend in deed.
He lives in a rich town.
Help yourself to the fresh vegetables.
As a matter of fact, he is very fat.
Ancient China is famous for its silk and china.
First come, first served.

4. Tongue twisters
He screams, she screams, they both scream for ice cream.
Six thick thistles sticks. Six thick thistles stick.
Ted sent Fred ten hens yesterday so Fred's fresh bread is ready already.
The man in black carried a map, a flag and a bag.
Terry Teeter, a teeter-totter teacher, taught her daughter Tara to teeter-totter .
The girl kissed her bird first.

I   Preview Exercises

1. Please say something about Christmas according to the following pictures.

What do you think of Christmas?

I think _____.

In my opinion, Christmas is _____.

My view is _____.

How do you usually spend Christmas?

First of all, _____.

Secondly, _____.

Finally, _____.

2. Please find out different expressions of Chinese people's attitudes towards the celebration of Christmas both positively and negatively.

II   Warming up Exercises

1. Look at the following pictures and tell us what you know about the dishes for dinner on Christmas Eve.

2. According to what you have heard in the listening course, nowadays Christmas becomes a non-religious holiday, do you think it is good or not?

3. What are the differences and similarities between Christmas and Spring Festival?

Listening Material Review

Directions: *In this section, you are going to listen to the material which you have heard in listening course again for several times. After finishing the first-time listening, you have to tell us what you have learned. After finishing the second-time listening, you should focus on important details and answer some specific questions in your own words. When it is played for the third and the fourth time, you should tell us what you think of this material. And at last you are required to listen and repeat several sentences in the material.*

Task 1

Questions for the first-time listening.

What is this material mainly about?

_____

Task 2

Questions for the second-time listening.

(1) Which word was used to describe Joseph in the passage? Do you think so? Why?

_____

(2) What does the sentence "the baby within her has been conceived by the Holy Spirit?" mean according to the angel?

_____

(3) When did the church leaders choose December 25th as Jesus' birthday?

_____

Task 3

🔊 *Questions for the third and the fourth-time listening.*

(1) What do you think of this material?

_____

_____

(2) Retell what the angel said to Joseph.

_____

_____

_____

_____

Task 4

🔊 *Now listen to the following sentences twice and repeat the whole sentences after you hear the sound of bell.*

(1) _____

(2) _____

(3) _____

(4) _____

Video-aural Material Review

Directions: *In this section, you are going to watch the video clip which you have done in listening course. After watching it for the first time, you have to tell us what you have learned. When you watch for the second time, you should focus on important details and answer some specific questions in your own words. When it is played for the third and the fourth time, you should tell us what you think of this clip. And at last you are required to listen to and repeat several sentences in the clip.*

Task 1

👁 *Questions for the first-time watching.*

What is this clip mainly about?

_____

Task 2

👁 *Questions for the second-time watching.*

(1) What are their impressions of Santa Claus?

_____

(2) What do you know about Saint Nicholas?

_____

(3) What did the French nuns do to the children?

_____

Task 3

👁 *Questions for the third and fourth-time watching.*

(1) What do you think of this clip?

_____

_____

(2) Retell what you have watched.

_____

_____

_____

_____

Task 4

 Now listen to the following sentences twice and repeat the whole sentences after you hear the sound of bell.

(1) _____

(2) _____

(3) _____

(4) _____

V Additional Video-aural Material

Directions: *In this section, you are going to watch an additional video clip. After watching it for the first time, you have to tell us what you have learned. When you watch for the second time, you should focus on important details and answer some specific questions in your own words. When it is played for the third and the fourth time, you should tell us what you think of this clip. And at last you are required to listen to and repeat several sentences in the clip.*

Task 1

Questions for the first-time watching.

What is this clip mainly about?

Task 2

👁 *Questions for the second-time watching.*

(1) What do you know about the first Thanksgiving from the passage?

_____

(2) Why did Pilgrims celebrate Thanksgiving with Indians?

_____

(3) Who gave thanks on this occasion? Can you tell us some of the names?

_____

Task 3

👁 *Questions for the third and fourth-time watching.*

(1) What do you think of this clip?

_____

_____

(2) Retell what they have been thankful for.

_____

_____

_____

_____

Task 4

🔊 *Now listen to the following sentences twice and repeat the whole sentences after you hear the sound of bell.*

(1) _____

(2) _____

(3) _____

(4) _____

VI

Phonetics Tips

Back vowels : [uː]—[u]　[ɔ]—[ɔː]　[aː]—[ʌ]

[u:]—[u]	1. 发后元音[u:]时需将双唇收圆,收小,并需要向前突出,在后元音中,[u:]的舌位最高,口形最小。发音时口腔肌肉始终保持紧张。 2. 后元音[u]的舌位比[u:]稍低,口形比[u:]稍大点,口腔肌肉放松,发短音。
[ɔ]—[ɔ:]	1. 发后元音[P]时口要张大,舌身平放后缩,双唇稍稍收圆,发短音。 2. 发后元音[P:]时舌后部抬得比[P]稍高。双唇要收得更圆更小,并需稍向前突出,发长音。
[a:]—[ʌ]	1. 发后元音[a:]时口要张大,舌尖离开下齿,舌身低平后缩,发长音。 2. 发中元音[ʌ]时口要张大,和前元音[æ]的开口程度相似,发短音。

Exercises:

1. Words

pool—pull	pot—port	park—puck
kook—cook	tot—taught	march—much
fool—full	cot—court	staff—stuff
stewed—stood	shot—short	heart—hut

2. Phrases

go to the zoo	a lot of shops	park the car
full moon	eat a hot dog	a hard task
a good-looking woman	four horses	ugly buckling
look at the book	walk on the lawn	touch the button

3. Sentences

I ate some noodles at noon.

Good cooking can't be learned from cookbooks.

Bob forgot to lock the door.

In the north of China, autumn is very short.

After parking the car, he disappeared in the dark.

There are enough drugs to support the area which is suffering from floods.

4. Tongue twisters

Is it hard to toot, or to tutor two tutors to toot?

The woman could look at the book in the wood.

Fox knocked at the door to send the hot dog.

Mr. See owned a saw and Mr. Soar owned a seesaw.

The answer in the article will be discussed in the afternoon.

A skunk sat on a stump and thunk the stump stunk, but the stump thunk the skunk.

I

Preview Exercises

1. **Look at the following pictures and have a discussion on what we should do and what we should not do:**

For the purpose of ... I think:

We are not allowed to _____.

Human beings can't _____.

People shouldn't _____.

It's wrong for us to _____.

In order to ... I think we can do as follows:

We have to _____.

Human beings are supposed to _____.

People must _____.

It's compulsory for us to _____.

2. **Please find out some more ways of expressing your attitude toward environmental protection.**

_____

_____

_____

_____

II

Warming up Exercises

Look at the following pictures and answer the following questions:

1. How much do you know about our earth? What happened to her? Is she healthy or seriously ill? Why?

2. Can you find any actions that may destroy our environment in daily life? If you can, please give us some examples.

3. Suppose you are the doctor for environmental protection, how can you cure our mother earth?

Listening Material Review

Directions: *In this section, you are going to listen to the material which you have heard in listening course again for several times. After finishing the first – time listening, you have to tell us what you have learned. After finishing the second – time listening, you should focus on important details and answer some specific questions in your own words. When it is played for the third and the fourth time, you should tell us what you think of this material. And at last you are required to listen and repeat several sentences in the material.*

Task 1

Question for the first-time listening.

What are the key words which this passage develops around?

Task 2

Questions for the second-time listening.

(1) How to find a better way to reduce what you are using now?

(2) Can you give us some more examples about "reuse"?

(3) Have you ever recycled any items in you life? How?

Task 3

 Questions for the third and the fourth-time listening.
(1) What is your understanding of "reduce, reuse, recycle"?

(2) Retell the passage you have just heard.

Task 4

Now listen to the following sentences twice and repeat the whole sentences after you hear the sound of bell.
(1) _____
(2) _____
(3) _____
(4) _____

IV　　Video-aural Material Review

Directions: *In this section, you are going to watch the video clip which you have done in listening course. After watching it for the first time, you have to tell us what you have learned. When you watch for the second time, you should focus on important details and answer some specific questions in your own words. When it is played for the third and the fourth time, you should tell us what you think of this clip. And at last you are required to listen to and repeat several sentences in the clip.*

Task 1

👁 *Questions for the first-time watching.*

What is this clip mainly about?

_____

Task 2

👁 *Questions for the second-time watching.*

(1) Where are grass-roofs coming from?

_____

(2) What are the advantages of grass-roofs? Can you list some according to the video?

_____

(3) What is former U. S. president Bill Clinton's opinion about it? Does he agree or disagree with it? Why?

_____

Task 3

👁 *Questions for the third and fourth-time watching.*

(1) What do you think of this clip?

_____

_____

(2) Retell the message you have just watched.

_____

_____

_____

_____

Now listen to the following sentences twice and repeat the whole sentences after you hear the sound of bell.

(1) _____

(2) _____

(3) _____

(4) _____

V Additional Video-aural Material

Directions: *In this section, you are going to watch an additional video clip. After watching it for the first time, you have to tell us what you have learned. When you watch for the second time, you should focus on important details and answer some specific questions in your own words. When it is played for the third and the fourth time, you should tell us what you think of this clip. And at last you are required to listen to and repeat several sentences in the clip.*

Task 1

Questions for the first-time watching.

What is this clip mainly about?

Task 2

👁 *Questions for the second-time watching.*

(1) What happened to Susie's ice-cream?

_____

(2) Can you catch the meaning of the phrase " pop in " ? Will you make up some sentences with it?

_____

(3) How to understand the sentence "Thus, solving the problem once and for all. "? Will the problem be solved once and for all? Why?

_____

Task 3

👁 *Questions for the third and fourth-time watching.*

(1) What do you think of this clip?

_____

_____

(2) Retell the message you have just watched.

_____

_____

_____

_____

Task 4

🔊 *Now listen to the following sentences twice and repeat the whole sentences after you hear the sound of bell.*

(1) _____

(2) _____

(3) _____

(4) _____

VI Phonetics Tips

Diphthongs：［ei］,［ai］,［ɔi］,［əu］,［au］

Directions：*There are eight diphthongs in English. Diphthongs are sounds which consist of a movement or glide from one vowel to another. The first part of a diphthong is much longer and stronger than the second part.*

［ei］	1. 发双元音［ei］时口形由［e］向［i］滑动,发音过程中下巴稍向上合拢,舌位也随之稍稍抬高。 2. 所有的双元音(共 8 个)发音时都应该前重后轻,前长后短。
［ai］	发英语双元音［ai］时由舌位低、口形大的前元音［a］向舌位高、口形小的［i］滑动。发音时舌尖要抵住下齿。
［ɔi］	发双元音［ɔi］时由后、低元音［ɔ］向前、高元音［i］滑动,口形由开圆逐渐变为合扁。
［əu］	发双元音［əu］时口形由中元音［ə］向后元音［u］滑动,开始的口形是扁平唇,结束的时候是合圆唇。
［au］	发双元音［au］时由舌位低、口形大的前元音［a］向舌位高,口形小的［u］滑动。结束时的口形是合圆唇,双唇须向前突出。

Exercises：

1. Words

bay—buy—boy   bouts—boats

fail—file—foil   town—tone

tails—tiles—toils   fowl—foal

lanes—lines—loins   how—hoe

bail—bile—boil   loud—load

ail—isle—oil   noun—known

tay—tie—toy   now—know

cane—kine—coin   found—phoned

2. Phrases

make face	a nice night	a joyous boy
make a mistake	fly high	annoyed by the noise
shout out	Road Home	
about two hours	grow old	

3. Sentences

I'll have an umbrella in case it rains.

I can't afford to be late for the plane again.

I can see nine kites in the sky.

Why didn't you buy the bike?

The toy was destroyed.

The boy joined us and we enjoyed the dinner together.

Mother didn't allow me to go out.

Open your mouth and pronounce the word loudly.

He met an old man on the road.

It's only a joke.

4. Tongue twisters

Kate's aim is to know the baby's name.

In case of life, I just had a great time and I might never be able to find you again.

A noisy noise annoys an oyster.

The old man put his old yellow coat in the boat.

Our teacher is shouting at the cow in the playground now.

Preview Exercises

1. **Please say something about the opening ceremony of 2008 Beijing Olympic Games according to the following pictures.**

the footprints of history

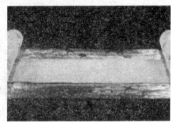

the scroll

the movable-type printing

the human Bird's Nest

There are various excellent performances in 2008 Beijing Olympic Games like the footprint, the human Bird's Nest, the Peking opera, etc. Which performance do you like best? Why? You may need to make comparison between the different performances.

Sample 1:

In my opinion, the performance of _____ is the most excellent one.

The reason why I think it is the most excellent one is that _____.

Sample 2:

Compared with other performance, I think _____ is much better than others.

It is because _____.

---

2. **Summarize ways of comparing the differences.**

II

Warming up Exercises

1. Please tell the differences between the ancient Olympic Games and the modern O-lympic Games according to the pictures and the information you know about the O-lympic Games.

2. Can you find some other differences which are not mentioned in the recording?
3. Check the preview exercise.

Listening Material Review

Directions: *In this section, you are going to listen to the material which you have heard in listening course again for several times. After finishing the first-time listening, you have to tell us what you have learned. After finishing the second-time listening, you should focus on important details and answer some specific questions in your own words. When it is played for the third and the fourth time, you should tell us what you think of this material. And at last you are required to listen and repeat several sentences in the material.*

Task 1

Questions for the first-time listening.

What is this material mainly about?

Task 2

🔊 *Questions for the second-time listening.*

(1) Who first used the motto? What did he/she use these words for?

_____

(2) Can you catch the meaning of the phrase "surpass himself"?

_____

(3) What is the meaning of the sentence "The Olympic Motto supposes the progress of human capacity on the basis of metal and physical improvement of man's natural qualities."?

_____

_____

Task 3

🔊 *Questions for the third and the fourth-time listening.*

(1) What do you think of the sense of the motto?

_____

(2) Retell the creed you have just heard.

_____

_____

_____

Task 4

🔊 *Now listen to the following sentences twice and repeat the whole sentences after you hear the sound of bell.*

(1) _____

(2) _____

(3) _____

(4) _____

IV Video-aural Material Review

Directions: *In this section, you are going to watch the video clip which you have done in listening course. After watching it for the first time, you have to tell us what you have learned. When you watch for the second time, you should focus on important details and answer some specific questions in your own words. When it is played for the third and the fourth time, you should tell us what you think of this clip. And at last you are required to listen to and repeat several sentences in the clip.*

Task 1

👁 *Questions for the first-time watching.*

What is this clip mainly about?

_____

Task 2

👁 *Questions for the second-time watching.*

(1) Who is Jacques Rogge? Can you give a brief introduction about him?

_____

(2) What is the meaning of the sentence "Where the sports performances of the highest possible level?" according to Rogge?

_____

(3) What do personal issues include according to Mr. Rogge?

_____

Task 3

👁 *Questions for the third and fourth-time watching.*

(1) What do you think of good organization?

_____

_____

(2) Retell the clip you have just watched.

_____

_____

Task 4

 Now listen to the following sentences twice and repeat the whole sentences after you hear the sound of bell.

(1) _____

(2) _____

(3) _____

(4) _____

V   Additional Video-aural Material

Directions: *In this section, you are going to watch additional video clip. After watching it for the first time, you have to tell us what you have learned. When you watch for the second time, you should focus on important details and answer some specific questions in your own words. When it is played for the third and the fourth time, you should tell us what you think of this clip. And at last you are required to listen to and repeat several sentences in the clip.*

Task 1

👁 *Questions for the first-time watching.*

What is this clip talking about?

_____

Task 2

👁 *Questions for the second-time watching.*

(1) When did volunteers first come to people's attention? And who are they?

_____

(2) Can you catch the meaning of the phrase "flag escorts"?

_____

(3) What does the sentence "They are very important and they are very helpful in many aspects of the organization." mean according to Mr. Rogge?

_____

Task 3

👁 *Questions for the third and fourth-time watching.*

(1) What do you think of the volunteers in the Olympic Games?

_____

_____

(2) Retell the video you have just watched.

_____

_____

_____

_____

Task 4

🔊 *Now listen to the following sentences twice and repeat the whole sentences after you hear the sound of bell.*

(1) _____

(2) _____

(3) _____

(4) _____

Phonetics Tips

The Correct Pronunciation of "ed", "es", "the"

The correct pronunciation of "ed"

Directions:

Rule 1: When a verb is ended with a voiceless consonant, "ed" is pronounced as [t].

Examples:

laugh—laughed	[lɑːft]	watch—watched	[wɔːtʃt]
kiss—kissed	[kist]	wish—wished	[wiʃt]
lock—locked	[lɔkt]		
help—helped	[helpt]		

Sentences:

He walked me to the bus stop and kissed me goodbye.

He looked at her and asked her to help him.

He stopped the car and locked it.

The teacher asked the boy to clean the window.

He helped her so she finished the work on time.

Rule 2: When a verb is ended with a voiced consonant or vowel, "ed" is pronounced as [d].

Examples:

cloth—clothed	[kləuðd]	rob—robbed	[rɔbd]
hang—hanged	[hæŋd]	beg—begged	[begd]
fill—filled	[fild]	rage—raged	[reiʒd]
open—opened	[əupənd]	close—closed	[kləuzd]
play—played	[pleid]	rain—rained	[reind]
fear—feared	[fild]	screw—screwed	[skruːd]
scan—scanned	[skænd]	burn—burned	[bənːd]

Sentences:

He got so angry that he yelled at me.

Mary closed the windows and left the classroom.

The students learned some English songs to perform.

The man who killed a panda was sentenced to death.

The little girl closed the window and cleaned it.

Rule 3: When a verb is ended with letter "t" or "d", "ed" is pronounced as [id].

Examples:

want—wanted	[wantid]	heat—heated	[hiːtid]
found—founded	[faundid]	joint—jointed	[dʒɔintid]

Sentences:

He recommended me for the job.

We boarded plane on time.

My mother wanted me to go by train.

Bob admitted he was wrong.

The correct pronunciation of "s" or "es"

Directions:

Rule 1: When a word is ended with voiced consonants, "s" is pronounced as [z].

Examples:

rob—robs	[rɔbz]	curtain—curtains	[kəːtns]
rug—rugs	[rʌgz]	telephone—telephones	[telifəuns]
room—rooms	[ruːmz]	word—words	[wəːdz]

Sentences:

He lives in a small town.

His clothes need new buttons.

These are the names and backgrounds of the persons.

There are two dogs in the garden.

He made some plans for the goals.

Rule 2: When a word is ended with consonants [s], [z], [tʃ], [ʃ], [dʒ], [ʒ], "es" is
   pronounced as [iz].

Examples:

mix—mixes	[mixiz]	difference—differences	[difərənsiz]
finish—finishes	[finiʃiz]	rose—roses	[rəuziz]
college—colleges	[kɔlidʒiz]	watch—watches	[wɔtʃiz]

The correct pronunciation of "the"

Directions:

Rule 1: When "the" is followed by a word which is initiated with a consonant, it is pronounced as [ðə].

Examples:

the car, the tree, the cat, the cup, the computer, the mirror, the light, the man, the woman, the bag, the ball, the bed, the match…

Rule 2: When "the" is followed by a word which is initiated with a vowel, it is pronounced as [ði].

Examples:

the ox, the old, the apple, the orange, the egg, the Europeans, the ostrich, the American, the Olympic…

I

Preview Exercises

Please say something about how you pay your tuition according to the following pictures.

Sentence Patterns
(1) Would you mind...
(2) Such as...
Would you mind telling me how many different ways you can pay your tuition?
No, _____.
There are different ways in helping our parents relieve financial burdens, such as
_____.

Sentence Pattern:
(3) Excuse me, could you tell me...?
Excuse me, could you tell me your understanding about the Green Channel?
Yes,
_____.

II

Warming up Exercises

1. Please tell us advantages and disadvantages of taking a part-time job.

www.educhn.net

2. **Please discuss and debate the advantages and disadvantages of taking a part-time job.**

Listening Material Review

Directions: *In this section, you are going to listen to the material which you have heard in listening course again for several times. After finishing the first-time listening, you have to tell us what you have learned. After finishing the second-time listening, you should focus on important details and answer some specific questions in your own words. When it is played for the third and the fourth time, you should tell us what you think of this material. And at last you are required to listen and repeat several sentences in the material.*

Task 1

Questions for the first-time listening.

What is this material about?

_____

Task 2

Questions for the second-time listening.

(1) What does the word "compensation" or phrase "feel free to" mean?

_____

(2) Can you catch the meaning of the word "brochure"?

_____

(3) What does the sentence "I will commend you to a follow-up interview with the sales manager." mean according to the female speaker?

_____

Task 3

 Questions for the third and the fourth-time listening.

(1) What do you think of this material?

_____

(2) Retell the conversation you have just heard.

_____

Task 4

 Now listen to the following sentences twice and repeat the whole sentences after you hear the sound of bell.

(1) _____

(2) _____

(3) _____

(4) _____

IV   Video-aural Material Review

Directions: *In this section, you are going to watch the video clip which you have done in listening course. After watching it for the first time, you have to tell us what you have learned. When you watch for the second time, you should focus on important details and answer some specific questions in your own words. When it is played for the third and the fourth time, you should tell us what you think of this clip. And at last you are required to listen to and repeat several sentences in the clip.*

Task 1

👁️ *Questions for the first-time watching.*

What is this clip about?

_____

Task 2

👁️ *Questions for the second-time watching.*

(1) Which of the three candidates seems to be eliminated?

_____

(2) What criteria do the two interviewers emphasize most?

_____

(3) What does the sentence "I think he has more charm than real leadership skills." mean according to the male speaker?

_____

Task 3

👁️ *Questions for the third and fourth-time watching.*

(1) What do you think of this clip?

_____

_____

(2) Retell the message you have just watched.

_____

_____

_____

_____

Task 4

🔊 *Now listen to the following sentences twice and repeat the whole sentences after you hear the sound of bell.*

(1) _____

(2) _____

(3) _____

(4) _____

Additional Video-aural Material

Directions: *In this section, you are going to watch an additional video clip. After watching it for the first time, you have to tell us what you have learned. When you watch for the second time, you should focus on important details and answer some specific questions in your own words. When it is played for the third and the fourth time, you should tell us what you think of this clip. And at last you are required to listen to and repeat several sentences in the clip.*

Task 1

👁 *Questions for the first-time watching.*

How many factors have been mentioned for an effective job hunting? What are they?

Task 2

👁 *Questions for the second-time watching.*

(1) What can you take in the job list?

(2) How can you seek help and advice from others when hunting a job?

(3) How do you understand the sentence "The best way to break this ambivalence is to organize your thought." according to the speaker?

Task 3

👁 *Questions for the third and fourth-time watching.*

(1) What do you think of this clip?

_____

_____

(2) Retell the message you have just watched.

_____

_____

_____

_____

Task 4

🔊 *Now listen to the following sentences twice and repeat the whole sentences after you hear the sound of bell.*

(1) _____

(2) _____

(3) _____

(4) _____

Phonetics Tips

Back vowels: [uː]—[u] [ɔ]—[ɔː] [ɑː]—[ʌ]

[uː]—[u]	1. 发后元音[uː]时需将双唇收圆,收小,并需要向前突出,在后元音中,[uː]的舌位最高,口形最小。发音时口腔肌肉始终保持紧张。 2. 后元音[u]的舌位比[uː]稍低,口形比[uː]稍大点,口腔肌肉放松,发短音。
[ɔ]—[ɔː]	1. 发后元音[ɔ]时口要张大,舌身平放后缩,双唇稍稍收圆,发短音。 2. 发后元音[ɔː]时舌后部抬得比[ɔ]稍高。双唇要收得更圆更小,并需稍向前突出,发长音。

215

[ɑ:]—[ʌ]

> 1. 发后元音[ɑ:]时口要张大,舌尖离开下齿,舌身低平后缩,发长音。
> 2. 发中元音[ʌ]时口要张大,和前元音[æ]的开口程度相似,发短音。

Exercises:

1. Words

pool—pull	pot—port	park—puck
kook—cook	tot—taught	march—much
fool—full	cot—court	staff—stuff
stewed—stood	shot—short	heart—hut

2. Phrases

go to the zoo	a lot of shops	park the car
full moon	eat a hot dog	a hard task
a good-looking woman	four horses	ugly buckling
look at the book	walk on the lawn	touch the button

3. Sentences

I ate some noodles at noon.

Good cooking can't be learned from cookbooks.

Bob forgot to lock the door.

In the north of China, autumn is very short.

After parking the car, he disappeared in the dark.

There are enough drugs to support the the area which is suffering from floods.

4. Tongue twisters

Is it hard to toot, or to tutor two tutors to toot ?

The woman could look at the book in the wood.

Fox knocked at the door to send the hot dog.

Mr See owned a saw and Mr Soar owned a seesaw.

The answer in the article will be discussed in the afternoon.

A skunk sat on a stump and thunk the stump stunk, but the stump thunk the skunk.

I Preview Exercises

1. Please list some sentences of earthquake and people's feeling on it.

> It's a kind of _____.
>
> It's the one that _____.
>
> I am concerned/ apprehensive about _____.
>
> I am nervous/ worried about _____.

2. Please use the sentences in the above grid to express your attitude toward earthquake.

II Warming up Exercises

1. Please describe Wenchuan earthquake by using what you've learned.
2. Can you find some other ways in describing the earthquake from the two

pictures?

3. Summarize ways in the above grid to express your attitude towards earth-quake.

Listening Material Review

Directions: *In this section, you are going to listen to the material which you have heard in lis-tening course again for several times. After finishing the first-time listening, you have to tell us what you have learned. After finishing the second-time listening, you should focus on important details and answer some specific questions in your own words. When it is played for the third and the fourth time, you should tell us what you think of this material. And at last you are required to listen and repeat several sentences in the material.*

Task 1

Questions for the first-time listening.
What is this material mainly about?

Task 2

Questions for the second-time listening.
(1) Where is the epicenter of Wenchuan county?

---

(2) Can you catch the meaning of the phrase "disaster relief work"?

---

(3) What happened in east Beijing after this big earthquake in Sichuan?

Task 3

Questions for the third and the fourth-time listening.
(1) What do you think of this material?

---

(2) Retell the material you have just heard.

_____

_____

_____

_____

Task 4

 Now listen to the following sentences twice and repeat the whole sentences after you hear the sound of bell.

(1) _____

(2) _____

(3) _____

(4) _____

IV   Video-aural Material Review

Directions: *In this section, you are going to watch the video clip which you have done in lis-*
tening course. After watching it for the first time, you have to tell us what you
have learned. When you watch for the second time, you should focus on important
details and answer some specific questions in your own words. When it is played for
the third and the fourth time, you should tell us what you think of this clip. And
at last you are required to listen to and repeat several sentences in the clip.

Task 1

👁 *Questions for the first-time watching.*

What is this clip mainly about?

_____

Task 2

👁 *Questions for the second-time watching.*

(1) Who has a greater awareness of vibrations in the ground, some animal species or human beings?

_____

(2) What does the phrase "low frequency sound waves "mean?

_____

(3) What were the members doing during the World Wildlife Fund-sponsored tour?

_____

Task 3

👁 *Questions for the third and fourth-time watching.*

(1) What do you think of this clip?

_____

_____

(2) Retell the message you have just watched.

_____

_____

_____

_____

Task 4

🔊 *Now listen to the following sentences twice and repeat the whole sentences after you hear the sound of bell.*

(1) _____

(2) _____

(3) _____

(4) _____

Additional Video-aural Material

Directions: *In this section, you are going to watch an additional video clip. After watching it for the first time, you have to tell us what you have learned. When you watch for the second time, you should focus on important details and answer some specific questions in your own words. When it is played for the third and the fourth time, you should tell us what you think of this clip. And at last you are required to listen to and repeat several sentences in the clip.*

Task 1

👁 *Questions for the first-time watching.*

What is this clip mainly about?

_____

Task 2

👁 *Questions for the second-time watching.*

(1) What was the engineer doing?

_____

(2) Can you catch the meaning of the phrase "weather the storm"?

_____

(3) Why did the engineers design better buildings?

_____

Task 3

👁 *Questions for the third and fourth-time watching.*

(1) What do you think of this clip?

_____

_____

(2) Retell the message you have just watched.

_____

_____

_____

_____

Task 4

🔊 *Now listen to the following sentences twice and repeat the whole sentences after you hear the sound of bell.*

(1) _____

(2) _____

(3) _____

(4) _____

VI   Phonetics Tips

Methods of counting syllable numbers.

1. Definition of a syllable: a syllable is a word part and the basic unit of English rhythm. English words can have one, two, three or even more syllables.

2. How to count syllable numbers?

Rule 1: Most of the time, we may know the syllable number of a word by counting the number of vowels in it. The number of the vowels is the number of the syllables in that word.

receive—[risiːv]	(2)	considered—[kənsidəd]	(3)
dictionary—[dikʃənəri]	(4)	because—[bikɔz]	(2)
correct—[kərekt]	(2)	important—[impɔtənt]	(3)

Rule 2: For some words, we can't define their syllable numbers only by counting vowels. Pay
   attention to the three consonants: [l], [m], [n].

bubble—[bʌbl̩]   (2)   tourism—[tuəri sm]   (3)

bottle—[bɔtl̩]   (2)   cousin—[kʌ zn]   (2)

little— [litl̩]   (2)   season—[siː zn]   (2)

3. Exercises: please count the number of syllables in every word and sentence.

(1) preferred   (   )   (6) documentation   (   )

(2) shaved   (   )   (7) qualification   (   )

(3) ordinary   (   )   (8) secure   (   )

(4) simple   (   )   (9) glasses   (   )

(5) oranges   (   )   (10) listening   (   )

(11) He is going to start a new busniess.   (   )

(12) George came first in the competition.   (   )

(13) Americans eat breakfast and lunch quickly.   (   )

(14) Getting messages and giving instructions to assitants.   (   )

(15) It outlasts any other fabric.   (   )

I Preview Exercises

1. Please watch this clip and tell something about it for at least 1 minute.

> This is a …
> How wonderful …
> That reminds me of …
> I'll never forget the time I …
> I was really excited about …
> What impressed me most is …

2. Please find out some more ways of expressing something happening in the past.

II Warming up Exercises

1. Please watch the following clip and tell us about the first space trip in China.

2. Can you tell us your own unforgettable experience?

3. Summarize ways of expressing the past, describing experience.

III Listening Material Review

Directions: *In this section, you are going to listen to the material which you have heard in listening course again for several times. After finishing the first-time listening, you have to tell us what you have learned. After finishing the second-time listening, you should focus on important details and answer some specific questions in your own words. When it is played for the third and the fourth time, you should tell us what you think of this material. And at last you are required to listen and repeat several sentences in the material.*

Task 1

🔊 *Questions for the first-time listening.*

What has happened according to the material?

_____

Task 2

🔊 *Questions for the second-time listening.*

(1) Where does the material come from?

_____

(2) Who delivered an important speech?

_____

(3) What activity will be performed by Chinese astronauts for the first time in outer space?

_____

Task 3

🔊 *Questions for the third and the fourth-time listening.*

(1) What's the main idea of the president's speech?

_____

_____

(2) Please tell the main points of the material.

_____

_____

_____

_____

Task 4

 Now listen to the following sentences twice and repeat the whole sentences after you hear the sound of bell.

(1) _____

(2) _____

(3) _____

(4) _____

IV Video-aural Material Review

Directions: *In this section, you are going to watch the video clip which you have done in lis-*
tening course. After watching it for the first time, you have to tell us what you
have learned. When you watch for the second time, you should focus on important
details and answer some specific questions in your own words. When it is played for
the third and the fourth time, you should tell us what you think of this clip. And
at last you are required to listen to and repeat several sentences in the clip.

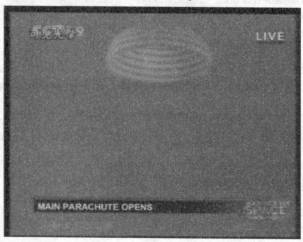

Task 1

 Questions for the first-time watching.

What does the picture show us?

_____

Task 2

👁 *Questions for the second-time watching.*

(1) Where did the astronauts stay when they were returning to Earth?

_____

(2) What's the biggest physiological problem at the moment the astronauts have just come back to Earth?

_____

(3) Who sent flowers to the astronauts?

_____

Task 3

👁 *Questions for the third and fourth-time watching.*

(1) Describe the pictures you have seen in your own words.

_____

_____

(2) Please retell what the first astronaut said.

_____

_____

_____

_____

Task 4

🔊 *Now listen to the following sentences twice and repeat the whole sentences after you hear the sound of bell.*

(1) _____

(2) _____

(3) _____

(4) _____

Ⅴ Additional Video-aural Material

Directions: *In this section, you are going to watch an additional video clip. After watching it for the first time, you have to tell us what you have learned. When you watch for the second time, you should focus on important details and answer some specific questions in your own words. When it is played for the third and the fourth time, you should tell us what you think of this clip. And at last you are required to listen to and repeat several sentences in the clip.*

Task 1

👁 *Questions for the first-time watching.*

What important information can you get from the clip?

Task 2

👁 *Questions for the second-time watching.*

(1) What is the suitable weather for the launching of the Shenzhou Ⅶ spacecraft according to the engineers?

(2) According to the story, what are the main parts of the Shenzhou Ⅶ?

(3) What can damage parts of the spacecraft which is transported according to the reporter?

Task 3

👁 *Questions for the third and fourth-time watching.*

(1) What can we learn from the video clip?

(2) Why did accompanying engineers keep a close eye on wind speed?

_____

_____

_____

_____

Task 4

🔊 *Now listen to the following sentences twice and repeat the whole sentences after you hear the sound of bell.*

(1) _____

(2) _____

(3) _____

(4) _____

VI   Phonetics Tips

Skills in reading the stressed syllables

1. What is a stressed syllable?

In words of the more than one syllable, one of them will receive more stress than the others. Stressed syllables are those that are marked in the dictionary as stressed. Stressed syllables are usully longer, louder, and higher in pitch.

Example:

chi	ne	se
syllable 1	syllable 2	syllable 3
(short)	(long)	(short)

> Stressed syllables:
> ※ are long
> ※ have a pitch change
> ※ have full vowel sounds

> Unstressed syllables:
>
> ※ are short
>
> ※ often have a reduced vowel sound

2. Three types of stress can be found in English: primary, secondary, and zero. The term **primary stress** refers to the strong emphasis a speaker puts on the most important syllable of a particular word. **Secondary stress** refers to a less strong emphasis on the next most important syllable. **Zero stress** refers to any syllable that receives no stress, such syllables are called **unstressed syllables.**

Example:

fe-male ['fiːmeil]   ex-am-i-na-tion [igˌzæmi'neiʃn]

3. Compound nouns normally have a primary stress on the *first element.*

   Compound proper nouns normally have a primary stress on the second element, except for the names of streets, like Forest Street.

   Examples:

   bathroom   daylight
   baseball   bookcase
   notebook   airport
   teenager   drugstore

   Good Friday   Wangfujing Street
   Easter Sundy   United States
   Beach Hotel   London Street

4. Exercises: Try to pronounce the following words correctly, pay attention to different syllabic stresses in them.

   resent   realistic   blackboard
   average   technician   sun glasses

necessity   communicate   White house
photographer   employee   bus stop
electrification   alcohol   traffic light
parental   forward   the Fifth Avenue
selfish   secretary   Wall Street
romantic   qualification   Atlantic Ocean
translator   interpreter   popcorn